A Book of Natures

Peter Kelly

'See that the imagination of nature is far, far greater than the imagination of man.'

Richard Feynman

Amazon Publishing

2023

No part of this publication may be reproduced, distributed, or transmitted in any form or by any means, including photocopying, recording, or other electronic or mechanical methods, or by any information storage and retrieval system without the prior written permission of the author, except in the case of very brief quotations embodied in critical reviews and certain other non-commercial uses permitted by copyright law.

Dedicado a mi amada y noble Paly, y a la hermosa línea de sangre que ha fluido de su ser: Alex, Kevin, Daniel, Sebastián, Bruno, y Max. Con amor y gratitud más allá del poder de mi pluma o labios para expresar plenamente.

Contents

Poems

Frozen Alive

Spellbound

A Love Poem

Bread and Water

Gate

Haiku

In Time

As One

Blackbird

Limbo

Haiku

Burglary

Shadows

Dawning

Dearest Tree

The Lyric Poet

Haiku

Death of a Dearest Friend

The Great Shadow

Seasons

To M

A Birth

Evening Time

Haiku

Father to Daughter

A Beautiful Child Twice Seen

Dryad

One Field Farm

Going In

Haiku

The Promise

Hymns

Epitaph

The Unknown Road

modern much poetry

Analogues

Visiting Mummy

Haiku

The Garden Speaks Volumes

The Impotent Bard

Haiku

Not Yet

Shelter from Inclemency

Threadbare

Too Late

Joie de Vivre

Wine

Short Stories

The Promise

Kindred Spirits

Nature's Course

The Compromise

Taking The Veil

The Gardener and The Prior

Turtle Dreams

Window on the Week

Still Forked

Poetry

'Set the foot down with distrust on the crust
of the world - it is thin.'

Edna St. Vincent Millay

Frozen Alive

Feet two arctic paws

hands ten freezer hooks

mouth a chattering cloud

nose two glacial floes

ears two witchy kisses

hair a tundra scape

Mind a blazing comet

Spellbound

Clouds billowed and pulled fleeting faces,

sunlit wings glittered in the afternoon air,

as he roamed and fathomed new places

among puddles and blossoms of plum

and rose in the orchard and petalful beds;

eyes up to the tweets from the tree tops,

and down for bumble and bluebottle hum.

The clouds merging to a sky overcast,

and his feet mottled with petal and mud,

meant his time in the garden had passed.

Her voice summoned him in for the hour,

a sound stronger, at first, than the sights.

Homeward, he held back for a moment

by a rose bush full out in flower.

Spellbound by the pink petals whirling,

he lingered long in their redolence,

till her voice overcame the enchantment,

leaving him passions as recompense.

A Love Poem

In a secluded street corner, just within reach

of the glow of a lone street lamp,

reposed a red rose,

its petals bowed down on the slender stem

shielded by weeds from a late frost and damp.

In the secluded street corner just out of sight

of windows and curious eyes,

a boy and girl stood

trembling with the thrill of their maiden kiss,

and adorning clichés with their ardent sighs.

In the secluded street corner, stark in the light

of the freshly initialed post,

the rose lay out flat,

crushed down on the earth by the errant feet

of two callow souls both by love engrossed.

Bread and Water

Your table is laid with beer and bread,

your mouth's wiped with

the cuff of your sleeve.

The rings on your fingers are

copper and brass,

your voice is as rough as hessian.

Your wife gave you ten; she can no more.

I offer you a slice and a glassful.

Your table is laid with wine and meats,

your serviettes are of

quality cotton.

The rings on your fingers are

silver and gold,

your voice is as posh as nylon.

Your wife gave you three; she said no more.

I offer you a loaf and a jugful.

Your table is laid with bubbly and game,

your napkins are of

finest silk.

The rings on your fingers are

diamond and gold,

your voice is as suave as velvet.

Your wife gave you none; you wanted four.

I offer you a baker and a wellful.

Gate

Open the gate to the field, my friends,
and we'll walk to the far-off grove.
My hands are too weak to cling to the stile,
so just let me through, if you would.

Close the gate to the field, my friends,
and we'll walk to the next in quiet.
My ears are too tired for any more talk,
so just to the next, if you would.

Open to the gate to the field, my friends,
and we'll sit ourselves by this hedge.
My sight is too dim to see what's in front,
so let me stop here, if you would.

Close the gate to the field, my friends,
to the car, for all is in vain.

My solipsism has overwhelmed me.

I'd go back on my own, if I could.

The lamb sucks at teat.

A bee returns spore ladened.

Winter! Oh winter!

In Time

Naked soil in rich clods sodden,
carved and upturned by steel, hoof and hand
toiling in age-old rhyme,
now settles to the lie of the land.

Thereafter, the once fallow field,
nurtured and worked by shower and shine
waking the life there sown,
will be clothed in golden folds, in time.

As One

As three, they slowly wandered
beneath the pine and ivy,
talking of lofty themes.
They heard the night wind swell.

As two, their voices faded,
for with each step their glances
won greater reach than sound.
They saw the moon a-sail.

Lying shy in deepening shade,
beneath the gown of the wood,
their breaths became as one.
They shared the earthy air.

Blackbird

(after Frost)

Out early one wet and gusty hour
to clear my head from a nightlong dream,
I left the road and walked the fields,
then reached a crag, beside a wood,
next to a gushing stream.

Rain fell in sheets and the thunder rolled
as I stood with my hands out turned.
No wing or paw would do the same
from bough up high, or burrow deep;
sense from the first birth learned.

Yet in a lull between clap and drop,
I heard a sound that gave me heart;

a blackbird in the wood unseen

had begun his song despite the storm.

It was due, and he played his part.

Limbo

His last was somewhere between

a rattle and snort.

His soul took quite a while to extract itself;

seemed reluctant, is what he thought.

At the Gates he wondered about

the oyster shells.

Doubts, of course, so questions were asked,

but the look on their faces always tells.

He answered, but his nose almost

half an inch grew.

A smirk and a shake of the haloed head.

"Good, but not squeaky enough.

Deary, you cannot go through."

A demon stood at the
just-below-melting-point gate,
as his soul hovered over the welcome mat.
"Another round of questions, mate."
Singed eyebrows were raised, a gentle
shake of the head;
his answers were a tad imprecise.
But those sweaty brows have never misled.
"Shabby, but not bad enough.
Damn it, but back up you go."
Up then down. Then up and back down again.
And as far as anyone knows,
he is still going to and fro.

Buddha swigged whisky.

Christ ate cake in the desert.

Books emit moonlight.

Burglary

I saw into your garden
by way of the gate,
which reminded me,
for it stood in the way
of my intruding in your home,

which I got into
by way of the window,
which reminded me,
for it was in the way
of my sneaking into your room,

which I saw into
by way of the door,
which reminded me,
for it got in the way
of my slipping into your bed,

which I got into

by way of your arms,

which reminded me,

for they lay in the way

of my breaking into your soul,

which I couldn't see into

by way of your eyes,

which reminded me of you,

for they blocked off the way

to me absconding with your heart.

Shadows

Alone I work, and with mottled hands
I clean the leaded glass.
About I see old friends are here,
the sanctified and the cursed,
all lying beneath the clay and grass.
No shadows at noon do they cast.

Alone they stand, green-grey mottled stones
with flowers at their base.
Engraved, they speak in terse cliché
of adult and child I have known,
bodies and souls my arms once embraced.
Their shadows cast long, since they passed.

Dawning

A new day slips
from the darkened hours,
and early light
sweeps through
the disarray of dreams,
and arcane fears are put to flight.

The warming rays
ascend the grey slate
roof and gravestones,
melting
the frost and midnight snow,
to beam out joys as yet unknown.

Dearest Tree

Dear, dearest tree,
how sentimental one can be
bewitched by such nobility.
Sat here beneath
your autumn splay of coloured leaf,
thus seems your proud and rugged bole
to stand with time entombed within.
Your whole is but the lives of kings
engrained within unnumbered springs.
Our history writ in cryptic rings.

But sentiment
has dulled the mind. I'll not relent.
This axe lays bare a keen intent.
A swift demise,
ordained by sacred fire, denies
the promise which the seed implied.

My needs demand
this sacrifice. Your wisdom soon shall be
as ashes cold and scattered free.

The Lyric Poet

When pensive minds are stirred to glance
at sunlight dawning on distant hills,
where warming airs pursue night chills,
and larks triple trill as they chirp and trance;

when stricken hearts are roused to gaze
at the yearning in twilit eyes,
once her breath has given to sighs,
heart beating bold as she swoons and sways;

then long the lyric bell will pour
out its rhymes in copper and gold.
Bewitchment by Earth and Heart told
from the poetry in sorrow and awe.

Children laugh at play,

while nightingales sing on high.

Why is He waiting?

Death of a Dearest Friend

When love falls short of distances,
like this that lies between us,
it takes slow leave of daily thoughts,
though still reposes in the heart,
weakened, since your depart.

With memory for sustenance
each autumn is a rebirth,
both of you then and of you now.
Thus owning yet denial lies
beneath a fragile, stoic guise.

The Great Shadow

See shadow and shade blend at the
speed of dusk to become
the Great Shadow of Night.
Hear pricklepin shuffle in hedgerows,
and the barn owl hoot from
a beam-lit bough.
See the sunflower slumber as the
moonflower exhales
in the still night air.
Watch the limbs of mighty oak and
ash unstrain and dip in
the nip of night.
Look as the mountain blooms
unfold to bring the purblind bat
and mottled moth.
Behold the moon and the steadfast
star lead wayfarers safely over

dune and wave.
Know in the Great Shadow of Night what
we cannot know in the dark of
the Great Light of Day.

Seasons

Winter greys afading
Spring returns athawing
Earth soon reawaking

Spring leaf buds abursting
Summer comes agreening
Flowers all abuzzing

Summer sun aburning
Autumn starts adaubing
Hedgerows all asinging

Autumn fields areaping
Winter chills acreeping
Earth soon re-asleeping

To M

In respect of an intimacy

forever to be implied,

a oneness of vision and song

by disparate journeys denied.

A Birth

Below a star riddled sky

and hand-sawn, oaken beams,

the tears that coursed her blushing face

paused at the side of her full-lipped mouth,

as she breastfed under the vacant gaze

of beasts breathing plumes in the icy air,

though she withheld her own till the stable

air was blessed by the newborn's breath.

Beneath pinpricked heavens, the stepfather

knelt at the side of the hand-hewn trough,

and tucked the child in his swathing cloth,

hands true to his noble vow, heart heavy with

doubt of the dream and her hand wrung pleas,

till he heard the questions to the elders put,

and of guests made merry on untrodden wine.

Evening Time

Recalled when day's toil is ended,
    fast aging hours flood in
    from the impending night.

In the fireside glow at twilight,
    the hearths of yesternights
    kindle in every hour.

The pen dreams poems.

The baton dreams symphonies.

Critics never sleep.

Father to Daughter

Every birdcall clear has rung,

all glow of the day is done.

The evening hours are now begun.

With a lover's smile

now run

to the web of love

he's spun,

for the inwoven breaths

now won,

as you lie with your hearts

undone,

and dream in your sleeps

as one,

till the dew disappears

in the sun,

and the time to return is come.

A Beautiful Child Twice Seen
(after Hardy)

Whilst standing in a waiting crowd,
I glanced upon your gladsome face
at the window of a passing car.
"Please stop!" I thought aloud.
While passing in a rushing crowd,
I glimpsed the sorrow in your eyes
through the window of a restaurant.
"Can't stop!" I thought aloud.

Had we but stopped and spoken,
about your smile, about your tear,
you would have bestowed on me
a happy heart and a haunted mind
for that day, and for many a year.

Dryad

A wanderer, not of this world, a girl
with green-brown eyes and ashen hair
passes by this night,
when storm clouds are unfurled.
I know this glorious, green-clad child a sprite,
one far roamed, in dire need
and greatly in despair.

No sounds or move I make; that barrier
no human voice, nor touch, can breach.
Her urgent gait,
the very sight of her,
speaks more than words could ever of fate
and tragedy. Her loss of ward lies beyond
what empathy can reach.

This unearthly child, not born to wander,
life-bound to leaf and sap and wood,
now walks alone
through thorn and thunder
in quest of groves of sturdy oak grown
far from cruel, unyielding winds
no withered tree withstood.

One Field Farm

Shame there were not two or more

each yielding their bountiful harvest.

Uncertain seed, unsown before,

sown in the furrows of a virgin earth,

meant little that ripened was reaped in full;

a crop stunted by plethora and dearth.

Better with fields abounding

to balance the bread with the stubble,

as a farm with only one field

is a farm that's asking for trouble.

Going in

The dewy stems yield as I lie
midst the poppy and chamomile.
Above and about, wings vivid
flit from bloom to bloom.
Each silken self a season manifest.
A greying cloud billows up high,
though slackens not to rain awhile.
About and beyond shut eyelids
warming rays illume.
Each petal lit, an image duly blessed.
Cool gentling airs pass by and by,
dispersing dust from daffodil.
Beyond and below, pools limpid
ripple neath the moon.
Each wavelet curls a naiad at its crest.

The snake sheds itself.

The woman sloughs her own child.

A rose is a rose…

The Promise

Dawn eased out from the hold of obscurity,

and slow dispersed cold vapours dense

with turbid thought and imagery.

Beams awoke the sunflower and honeybee,

and calm composed the promise rich

with birdsong and expectancy.

Hymns

As the horizon burns,
and the silhouetted oaks
revive as quivery leafflow,
breasty robin, peppered thrush,
and virtuosic blackbird
strike up from sprig and bough.

Wren flits and hops and trills
mid the languid coos of dove,
and at misty dawn of day
chattering finch and sparrow
dart among the leafy twigs,
and the witchy-black crow caws.

The day proclaims its glory
with sunlight full of cheer,

and less a morning chorus

than hymns for eye and ear.

Epitaph

Sing the carols I sang alone,

recite my verse, re-meet me there,

and read my dog-eared tomes.

Enter the woods where I was embraced,

heed the wisdom from feather and fur,

and follow the paths my longings traced.

Probe my friends and pry my foes,

drink deep of my whiskey and wine,

and unearth the roots of my drunken woes.

Plumb the depths of your heart and mind.

Look for me, I am there.

The Unknown Road

Across gleaming pools of light we walk,
hand in hand, not heart to heart.
Hopes stray far in the forest night,
as I gaze upon a pale and unknown road.

Beneath soughing in the pines we talk,
word on word, not lip on lip.
Thoughts drift far in the faint starlight,
as I gaze upon a pale and unknown road.

Upon beds of autumn leaves we lie,
side by side, no more as one.
Dreams recede till out of sight,
as I gaze upon a pale and unknown road.

modern much poetry lacks

Rhyme

        and Rhythm

and is Oft the lines of a paragraph or two

plonked from

⬆

to

down

to avoid

looking like an undergrad thesis on Dung Beetle Coprology.

(After e e modern poetry cummings)

If you're lucky

it may be p e p   p e r   e d

with

a Metaphor

there and   here,

but dipped in the teacup of Meaning

it leaves the best of it to drown

below.

Something your digestive biscuit might know.

Analogues

Doubt to belief is as courage to venture

Africa to Europe is as nest to cuckoo

Deeds to savings is as horizon to here

Truth to mind is as clay to potter

Poetry to awe is as cherry to blossom

Love to classroom is as heat to kitchen

Fear to bravery is as furnace to steel

Memory to past is as prophesy to future

Visiting Mummy

He stood confronting the house.
A lamp-lit room, a jaundiced eye,
stared out at the dark.
As old as the bricks,
she was reared and wedded there,
and after his unwelcome conception,
begrudgingly weaned him
and witnessed him beat a retreat.

Widowing herself, she settled into
pale cream sherry, and stoking her disdain
of her neighbours' lives
from the lace-lined, latticed window.

The gate creaked. Approaching he readied
his knuckles, but she heard and was there
as they met the wood.

A limp hug in the doorway
and a sidewards stare,
as she shuffled him through,
and past the room
where the memory of his father lurked,
to the lamp-lit room where she wove her
platitudes and specious claims
into a tattered rag, during tea.

Her mother suckled her, she suckled him;
four teats withered before lips were clamped.

The cup was still warm
when the gate creaked.
"Bye-bye, darling, don't be a stranger,"
her voice sliced through
the stillness of the night.

Leaving her street for the final last time,
he walked into a past where she would be less
than a memory of a memory
of a childhood dream.

Christ is expletive.

Buddha is jade souvenir.

Yew tree roots deepen.

The Garden Speaks Volumes

The flowers of season and soil,

trees of the wind and clime,

coo and caw of mood,

shadow and odour of the hour.

The Earth speaks to herself,

each utterance clear and true.

No breeze, or bloom, or birdcall,

a syllable beyond the sense.

The Impotent Bard

He has no itch,

no swelling of desire,

nothing approaching a climactic twitch.

There is no growth

from seed to ripe old age,

or unwanted birth.

Though he often gives forth

to big, bouncy poemlessnesses

that are dead and of no worth.

Lion shares my bed.

Thunderstorms cup in my hand.

Tomorrow unnerves.

Not Yet

Though leaves in autumn rust
and midst their boughs decay
ere pallid winter's disarray,
this, in spring, we will not know.

Though joys of childhood days
must fade to fabled rhyme
as innocence with age declines,
this, as babes, we cannot know.

Though overflowing hearts
may ebb to discontent,
sighs proving then the love misspent,
this, in love, we need not know.

Shelter from Inclemency

There is a place as real to my mind
as any ever seen.
One enchanted with sweetened airs,
soft grasses underlying
an ancient fount, and old stone walls
by a statue dappled green.
A place of peace and harmony with
padded paw, and wing.
The gentle rains oft falling there refresh
the gushing brook.
The sky spreads out above the grove,
marbled in grey and blue,
wistful reeds and willow trees swish
back and forth when shook.
In flight from storms, I call her forth
for the peace that I pursue.

Threadbare

Slow in changing to darkest threads,
for twilight grey yet lingers,
sedulous Saturn weaves the night
with gnarly, arthritic fingers.
With godly ease the darksome hours
are weft into human sleep,
and deftly the warps of dreaming
are, by Morpheus, threaded deep.

The final strands of night run through,
the pattern appears but dim.
Dull shines the moon with stolen beam
on Earth awhirl in regions grim.
Thus concluded, this woven night
is hung for eternity,
and Saturn, content, now ceases,
desiring this their end to be.

As always has and surely will,

despondency's foe puts right.

A single thread by Cupid pulled

bares Aurora bathing in light.

Too Late

The airs at dawn less gently fluff
red robin's feathered breast,
than how your untold love would have
troubled, once confessed.

Had you ventured from lands afar,
despite her weakened ken,
her tardy blood, her heart ajar
would have thrilled again.

Joie de Vivre (or Nothing Lasts)

It's in the…

zest of a succulent lemon

(before the rind spots black).

forest floors mantled in tulips

(till a late frost sets in).

cornfields engilding in sunshine

(then the sickle and scythe).

chicken brooding her eggs

(before the omelette is served).

mother bird feeding her nestlings

(ere the cuckoo is hatched).

foxes at play in the hedgerows

(prior to the baying).

lambs frollicking in the meadow

(till it's time for a Sunday roast).

artist holding true to herself

(ere the critics opine).

love and peace for one and all

(before the liver rots).

being, but more the becoming

(prior the final knell).

Wine

Ripened on latticed, southerly slopes,
its progeny
heavy clustered hung,
the slothful vine
is reaped by lusty hands.

Glorious joys and melancholy
are fermented
with the dusky grape.
Then honest wine's
uncorked upon us all.

The nectar now does wayward sway
thrust up by the tilted flow.
Palms curve gently the full-bodied glass,
slowly filling with bacchic Bordeaux.

The musty sea-red wine, now poured,
    allures the temperate soul
    with pseudo-oenological sips,
    till the bottle loses all control.

Short Stories

'Who looks outside, dreams; who looks inside, awakes.'

Carl Gustav Jung

The Promise

"Here! Stop…stop! I saw it over there."
The excitement in her voice convinced him. He pulled over and parked off the road and they got out. She pointed over the hedge towards the far side of the field, as he buttoned her cloak and pulled the hood over her head. He stood for a few seconds looking about; the early morning light cast a pale clarity onto the white fields ahead, but there were red embers around the upper edges of dark clouds above the woods. He wondered if they would have time. Crows flew in and out of the treetops, as their caws echoed across the fields. The wind suddenly rose and dusted up the freshest fall of the early hours.

Their boots crunched on the snow as he led the child from the roadside gate across to the next, her gloved hand snug inside his, and her thin, stockinged legs all angles in her effort to keep up with his strides. She said nothing, but he knew. He lifted her up, and his feet sank a little deeper as he continued to fulfil his promise.

As they neared the next field, the girl started to pat his shoulders to make him go faster, and he pretended to trot as best he could.

"It's not here," she said, when they reached the gate. Large snowflakes had begun to fall steadily and she reached out to catch some.

"Maybe the next one. Please!" she cried, tapping her heels into his sides.

"Tomorrow," he said. "Let's try again tomorrow."

"No! You promised!"

He brushed the snow from his face and looked. He could barely see more than halfway across the next field, but he knew the gate was straight ahead.

"OK. Just one more gate."

Her weight and his deepening steps took their toll, and it took him longer than he expected to cross the field. Halfway over, he felt his chest beginning to ache, and his legs weaken, but as he reached the far side of the field a sudden shrill scream of joy rang out from above. He stopped and looked up. There, silent and still, stood the mare the child had seen the previous day. The horse did not move. Her head hung over the iron gate and her eyes half closed against the increasing flakes, she exhaled warm, white fog into the air. The man and girl watched in silence, he alert to the approaching storm, she, oblivious to all except the huge, unmoving beast three steps ahead. Sensing her impatience, he eased her off his shoulders, and she sank to the top of her boots in the snow. She did not take his hand, but remained beside him, elf-like. In the stark, midwinter quiet, the three figures stood at the gate, as if painted onto the scene.

She took those three steps remarkably quickly, and was beneath the heavy head before he realised. The snow seemed to slow in its descent. Through it, he watched as the girl raised her tiny, gloved hand and patted the bristled jowl, and he saw the thick, blistered lips curl back from the jutting, yellow teeth as the mare first opened and then closed her mouth over the proffered hand.

"Saffron!"

The sound of his own voice jolted him, and he woke to what was happening. He reached the mare and girl in one stride. Aware that he did not know how to make a horse open its mouth, he grasped the child by the waist and lifted her up closer to the animal.

"She's hungry!" he heard her say, as he wrapped one arm around her and moved his other hand towards where her lower arm disappeared into the old mouth. The horse snorted out great jets of steam into their faces. Without thinking, he blew hard back into the mare's face, and he heard the girl giggle. The horse suddenly opened its mouth, releasing the wet gloved hand, and threw its head back and neighed sharply. He stepped back with her limp body dangling from his arm and set her down on the snow. Her knees bent until she stiffened her legs and then stood, staring at the horse.

He took off her glove and looked at her hand.

"Poor little thing! She wanted my glove!"

He looked back at the mare. It was walking away from the gate, and its unkempt, limp tail quickly disappeared in the squall that now surrounded them. He turned, but could barely make out the way back to the car. Taking her hand, he looked at it again, before wiping the saliva off the glove.

"You're OK," he said. "Put it on, we must hurry!" He picked her up and cradled her, as she wrapped her hood about her head as well she could. The storm was now fully upon them.

With her small body held snug against his, and her trusting eyes smiling up at him from between the folds of her cloak, he trudged firmly, knowing that there was little time left before he lost all orientation. Finally, staggering under the onslaught of relentless snowfall and her weight, he reached the roadside. He opened the car and gently sat her on the back seat, brushed the snow from her cloak and shut the door. Shaking off snow, and fear that he later denied, he walked round and wiped the windscreen with his forearm, kicked off the snow stuck to his boots, and climbed inside to catch his breath. In silence, he rubbed his thighs while he watched the windows mist up as the snow, now easing, flecked the other side of the glass. He felt in his pocket for the key.

"Time to go," he said. "They'll be worrying."

He has long forgotten what happened before they

had ventured out that morning, and little memory remains of what happened after they returned, but he still clearly remembers that journey back in the car; she smiling at him and he pulling faces at her in the rear-view mirror.

And he remembers her suddenly grinning and holding out her little red glove, saying, "are you hungry?"

Kindred Spirits

She approached just before closing time and gently laid two books on the counter.

"These two, please."

She was short, a bit older than she looked, and kept very much to herself. She had worked along side me in the library for nearly a year, and most every Thursday night she took out two books and returned them the following Monday.

"New topic, I see."

Normally, she took out historical stuff or short stories. The books in front of me were on Spiritualism.

"Yes…something new."

"Cool…know nothing myself. Maybe one day we can have a coffee and you can tell me all about it."

Karla was very attractive.

"Yes…maybe."

I registered the books, handed them to her, and she left. I checked no one else was inside, closed up, and before going home, I went for a drink.

Next morning I arrived a little late, and there was already a queue of one outside. That person, an elderly woman, an avid reader and complainer, turned towards me waving a book as I neared the door.

"It's six minutes passed!" she hissed.

"Yes, I know, dear. Sorry, won't happen again. Had a spot of trouble getting up."

She wavered, grunted and returned to her spot. She'd been expecting a lie and was ready to do battle. She would've lost.

The chief librarian was taking a long weekend off, so once Karla arrived we had the place to ourselves, so to speak.

"Started them yet?"

"Yes, but I want to ask something of you."

"Sure."

"I've been invited to some sort of do tonight, something special, and I want you to come with me."

By the way she put it, I couldn't decide if I was being asked out on a date or not, so I asked what sort of do it was.

"Well, it's not a do really, it's a spiritualist meeting, and a séance."

"Oh! Well…sorry, not really my thing."

"I know, but please…come."

Trying to hide my disappointment, and surprised by her insistence, I searched for something to say.

"Hmm…I mean, if it's not a party, surely you can go alone, or with a friend?"

She shook her head slowly, but I felt she wasn't answering me.

"Look, I know we just work together, but come with me, please."

I suddenly remembered what seances were all about. Maybe she just wanted some support.

"I didn't know you lost someone. I'm sorry to hear that."

She just looked at me.

"Please…just for a while."

She picked me up outside the library just before 7:15 that evening, and we drove out of town, in silence most of the way. After five minutes or so, she turned into a small lane that ran below the barley fields on either side. The signpost at the corner said 'Northvale Manor 2 miles'.

"Really?"

"Yes, but I don't know them. I saw something in the paper about a spiritualist group and enquired. They responded with an invitation to a session."

"I think they call them mediums… or media?" She didn't laugh. She seemed distracted.

Northvale Manor was the abode of the local, retired army man, the 'Colonel' as he was called, and his wife. They owned the local hunt. Rumour had it he wasn't a real colonel; some doubting Thomas in the village had looked in the service records. His wife was very young.

The tall gates to the estate were open when we arrived, and Karla drove through and slowed down in the yard outside the main entrance. The tyres on the gravel made a long crunching sound as we stopped. Several Landrovers and Jeeps were already parked round a central fountain. As we got out, a woman opened the front door and approached us with open arms.

"You must be Karla! So glad you could come. And you did bring your friend. Excellent!"

"Yes, this is Andrew. We work together." Exuberant greetings: hugs for Karla and clasped hands for me.

"I'm Dolly, not my real name but everyone calls me that. Colonel Granger is my husband. Please, come this way."

We were led into a large, dimly lit lounge where over a dozen people were sitting in an oval formation. There were few empty seats. Dolly showed us to ours and then went and sat next to what I assumed was her husband a few places to our left. I noticed the empty seat opposite us was an old, purple and gold threaded, leather armchair.

I looked around. Roughly an even number of late middle-aged men and women made up the majority of the group. Only Karla and I and two others were much younger. The room had a floor to ceiling library at one end, and vast portraits hung from the other three walls. Everything was lit by soft, yellow wall lamps.

My eyes came to rest on the figure of the colonel. He was wearing jodhpurs and he was staring at me. I nodded slightly. He didn't. Neither of us smiled.

He stood and began to address the group. He welcomed each member one by one; Dolly must have given him our names. As he introduced us, he paused. For the second time that night I felt coming might be a mistake. He continued by informing everyone that the medium was on his way. He had just arrived from India and was coming directly from the airport. There were one or two murmers of excitement. Dolly nodded, as she looked about wide-eyed.

I felt Karla's hand rest on my arm. I turned, she looked pale in the lounge light. Her lovely eyes were focussed on the low table in front of her.

Once he had finished, the Colonel sat and everyone settled into small groups to chat and wait. Karla and I said nothing to each other and were ignored by the others. I was only aware of her hand on my arm.

"He's here!" exclaimed Dolly. She stood up and walked briskly to the door. She returned arm in arm with what looked like a middle-aged accountant.

Some greying hair hanging over one side of his forehead suggested the wind had picked up outside, or a touch of vanity. His suit was rumpled. He stood in front of the empty armchair and smiled at us all. It was a startling smile, disconcerting in its odd intensity.

People were half way up, when he said, "Please, sit everyone. I'm so, so happy to be here."
As I tried to get more comfortable, I realised Karla had removed her hand.

"You OK?"

"Fine, thanks. Just a bit nervous, maybe. You?"
I smiled and shrugged, and immediately wished I hadn't. Despite my reservations, I wanted her to know I was here for her.

Tea was brought in by two silent housekeepers. As they went round serving, one of the younger men stood and blurted, "I saw someone's spirit come in with you! Faintly, but he was there, just behind you." No one seemed surprised, no murmers or gasps. It was as if he had said he saw one of the hounds pad in. The medium said nothing, but just clasped his palms together vertically in front of his chest and bowed slightly. I lowered my head to hide my growing suspicions.

"Did you see him?" The Colonel was standing in front of me with a plate of biscuits in one hand.

"Afraid not."

He gave a knowing nod and stepped away. He didn't offer a biscuit to either of us.

The cups and saucers were collected, and a silence ensued. All eyes were turned to the occupant of the armchair. In a firm but beguiling voice, he began by relating his visit to India and briefly summarised his experience with a 'great guru'. It all sounded rather anachronistic to me. He repeated how glad he had been to get the invitation to conduct this evening's séance with us all. So glad, in fact, he had cut short his trip and booked the next flight back. Discretly looking at the miscellany of figures in the group, I found that hard to believe. 'Séance' he had said. It was the first time the word had been mentioned since we arrived.

He continued.

"Before we all move to the other room to start, I want to first welcome your two new guests, if I may, Dolly. You've very kindly accepted them into your little group and that makes me very happy."

Dolly smiled, and almost wriggled in her chair.

I felt Karla's hand on my arm again.

He turned to her.

"Welcome, Karla. I can see it's your first time here, or possibly in any session. I'm right, aren't I?"

She nodded.

"Very good. I know you Karla, I understand. Have we met before?"

"No."

"Do you believe I know you?"

She didn't answer, but looked steadily at him.

"You have your reasons for being here, and one is obvious, but the other isn't, is it? You keep it a secret, but I can see your truth that scares you."

I looked at him. He was focussed on Karla. Everyone was.

"You haven't told anyone. And that's what scares you…telling people…that you are gay."

Something exploded within me. I rose abruptly.
"What the hell!"

"He doesn't believe. He shouldn't be here!" The colonel was standing, pointing at me.

Noise erupted.

The man in the armchair slowly stood and motioned for quiet.

"Am I right, Karla?"

I looked at her. Her breath shuddered, but she was still looking straight at him.

"This is not right! How dare you!" I took half a step towards him.

He looked at me.

"I know you, too, Andrew."

I stood still.

"The hell you do!"

"Andrew, please, sit. Please." That smile again.

I felt Karla squeeze my arm more tightly pulling me back.

I looked at her.

"Please, sit," she said.

I sat, and put my hand over Karla's. She put her other hand on top of mine. I turned to face him.

"Here, in our group," he continued, "everyone's truth must be faced, Andrew. It's hard I know. But it's way too easy to live the lie. If the living don't live by their truths, they can't heal, they can't be true to themselves, and the spirits won't reach out. You're angry now, very angry, but that feeling is not unusual for you. You have trouble in not letting your great anger spill out onto the world. You've even seriously considered hurting people. That is your truth, Andrew. And you tell yourself it's the world that makes you angry. That's your lie. The one you tell yourself every night."

"This is bullshit!"

I stood and pulled Karla up "Let's go!"

"Yes, leave! I knew you didn't belong here. Dolly, why on earth…"

Dolly had her hands clasped together and seemed to be pleading with her husband.

Several rose in an attempt to calm things down. Karla seemed unsure and hung back, but I was adamant. "We're leaving, come on."

The medium looked at me without smiling. On our way out, I heard him invite the others to the next room.

I opened the passenger door for Karla and she got in. I felt she was in no state to drive, and I insisted. As I climbed in, Dolly came rushing up. "I'm so, so sorry, the colonel gets very upset. I'm sure it'll be better next time. Please come again, both of you." She nodded as she smiled at Karla.

I thanked her for both of us and she withdrew her face from the window. As I drove out, I noticed a silver and black Rolls parked near the fountain. The inside light was on. Two men were reading the newspaper.

I drove all the way back keeping to the limit; I was in no mood to argue with any police. Karla said nothing, but she gave way to tears once. My outrage had given way to anger and pity. He had no right to do that to her, or me. I drove to my place, parked and got out. She shuffled over into the driver's seat, lowered the window and rested her arm there. Her eyes glistened in the street light. She looked very tired.

"I'm sorry," she said. "But I'm very glad you went."

Shaking my head, I patted her arm gently. I stood back and watched her slowly drive off.

Inside, I poured myself a drink and sat on the bed. Questions about the evening whirled in my head, but thoughts about what had happened were constantly edged out by thoughts about Karla. I could still feel her hand on my arm, see her face. Once in bed, I recalled the medium's last words. Shortly before I fell asleep, I began wondering whether that man might be right about her. I knew he was right about me.

The following Monday we both arrived at the same time. Unlocking the door, I let her in and we went about our business without speaking. At one point she had left her books in the trolley, and I went to the aisle to return them. She was there taking out another book. We looked at each other.

"Is it true, what he said about you?" I asked.

"Yes, oh yes. And what he said about you?" she asked. She was looking at me, observing me. Her hand was back on my arm. She seemed different, very confident.

"Yes, maybe."

I heard someone at the front put some books down. She looked at me for a while in silence.

"Will it be better next time?" I heard myself say.

"Oh, I think so," she said, smiling, and she gently patted my arm before walking back to the front desk.

Nature's Course

The party had finished, and the hum of their parents chatting in the kitchen could be heard from the porch where Jane and her older sister, Philippa, were sitting looking out over the snow covered lawn.

Close friends and cousins, antique aunts and hungry uncles had mingled with the children and their parents in the living room all morning. Jellies and cakes had mingled with assorted sandwiches on the table below the window. A few semi-deflated balloons, coloured streamers and pointy, paper hats were still scattered around. Today, Jane had turned twelve, and she had spent the morning playing games and chatting and laughing around the table. All the guests had left, and after a half-hearted attempt at clearing up, Philippa and Jane had sneaked out to the porch. Philippa was sat on the floor trying to squeeze down the last of the neatly cut cheese and cucumber sandwiches. Jane was on the couch holding a glass and sipping the last of the juice with a gurgling sound.

"You're going to pop if you eat that," she said.

"Do you have to slurp so much?" responded Philippa.

Jane slurped louder and laughed, but they were suddenly interrupted by a shout from the kitchen.

"Jane, come quick!"

They both raced to the kitchen where their parents were pointing to Molly's basket beneath the table. Molly was in it lying on her side and suckling two white kittens, while a black and white one was blindly trampling over them to get to its fair share.

"Look, Jane. Three!"

Jane let out a whoop, knelt and lifted out the black and white kitten and it moved drunkenly in her cupped palms, mewing sharply.

"She's so cute!" she said, as she gently stroked the soft damp fur around the kitten's chin. It purred noisily.

She picked up the other two and held all three to her chest. Molly got to her feet and began rubbing against Jane's knees.

"She's purring too."

"Well, yes, she's now a mummy," her father said, kneeling beside her. "Let's put them back in the basket. Molly's going to clean and feed them and you can watch, but I think we should let her do what she needs to do. Let nature take its course, Ok? Tonight you can take them all up to your room. Pretty good timing, I think!"

Jane returned all three, doing her best to align them neatly, and then began to fuss about them being warm enough, having enough milk, and to wonder if any more would be arriving. Her parents let her be. She had never experienced another's birth before.

"Lunch will be soon," her father said. "You two can keep watching till we call you."

At lunch, Jane sat with the black and white kitten on her lap.

"This one's my favorite," she said, stroking the crown of its head. "I'm going to call her Milly."

"How do you know it's a she?" said Philippa.

"I'll check later," said their mother. "They're a bit young."

"If it turns out to be a boy you could call him Billy. Close enough," said Philippa.

Once lunch was over, they cleared up what remained of the party and then put on warm clothes and boots and left the house for their Sunday walk. Jane got to choose where they would go, and she decided on a walk through the nearby woods, where she hoped to see the bluebells.

"Then we could pop in to see Grandpa, as he couldn't come," she said.

A short way into the woods, Philippa suggested they split up and take different paths, all of which led to the other side of the wood and close to where their grandfather lived. Jane and her father went off together, and her sister and mother took a separate path.

Chatting and half skipping, she pulled on her father's hand, impatient to get to the bluebells. He had hoped to take the chance to teach her a little about kittens, but quickly abandoned the idea of getting any such ideas passed her excitement.

"There they are!" she cried, running to the base of a large thicket where the violet-tinged flowers were poking up through the crusty snow.

"I want to pick some for Grandpa. I'll catch up in a minute."

Her father said he would wait for her by the next fork in the path.

Opening a pocket in her jacket, she knelt and began picking the firmest and placed them gently inside. Standing up in order to look for more, she became aware of faint sounds over to her right. From where she stood, she couldn't make out what it might be, and so took a few steps deeper into the thicket and listened; something was making faint high-pitched sounds further ahead. In the still quiet of the winter's day the sounds were eerie. She tentatively stepped forward, but her boots on the frosted snow made far more noise than she wished. She stopped again. Whatever it was appeared unperturbed by her approach.

After a few more steps, the sounds were now clearly tiny screams. Startled, she realised the sounds were coming from just ahead to her right, and she was near enough to see, but for a low, snow-laden branch. Controlling herself, she carefully drew the branch aside with one arm and looked.

Instantly stricken by the scene, she froze, her mouth open but her throat closed against any scream. Two tiny kittens were squealing and hobbling round and round the area outside the entrance to the warren, amidst an intense scene of ruin.

Bright red blood was melting snow; a large irregular crimson patch, like a vivid birthmark, lay in front of the burrow, and smaller carmine blotches were scattered to the right of the opening. Other kittens, some still twitching, lay strewn around the whole stage, throats gashed. Fending off low twigs with her forearms, she took a few half-crouched strides to where two more kittens were limping in deranged circles around clumps of fur, and where brighter splotches led away from the burrow. The author of such ruin had left with the doe.

Jane stood rigid above the carnage with her hands on either side of her head, her mouth still open in shock.

She suddenly heard the crunch of footsteps behind her and felt a hand on her shoulder.

"You ok?" but he stopped at the sight.

"Oh my goodness! I thought you were hurt. Oh, Jane!" He turned her round to face him.

"What can we do, dad? We must do something!" she managed to say.

"There's nothing we can do. Come on, I know it's hard, but we should get going. Let...let nature take its course."

Leading her out of the thicket, he hugged her tightly and let her sob. When she had stopped, he held her face in his hands and told her to breathe deeply.

"Such a shame," he said. "But let's go and see Grandpa now."

Although she had been in no danger, she now felt safe, and said she just wanted to stay for a minute before they carried on. As they stood on the path, he with his arm round her shoulder, pigeons cooed from the branches above them, and partridge wings thudded and thrummed through the air further along. A breeze sprang up from nowhere unsettling the snow on the branches, and beyond the tree tops they could see a hawk hovering high in the grey. Something like a dog bark, triumphant, came from a short way off.

She hugged him. "Ok," she said.

In silence they carried on along the path. When they caught up with her sister and mother, Jane hugged her mother and showed her the bluebells.

"Why the tears?" her mother said, staring at her and frowning.

"She's just seen what a fox can do," he said.

Her mother gave her another hug, as she looked at her husband. He shrugged. Then looking at Philippa, she put a finger over her own lips. Philippa nodded.

At her grandfather's house, Jane put the now wilting flowers in a vase with water, and during much of the time there kept looking at them hopefully. She thanked her grandfather for the gift he had sent over, and then Philippa told him all about Molly and her kittens.

"Oh how lovely! How lucky you are she gave birth on your birthday, Jane," he said. "That was her present to you. I remember when this cat was born, and your grandmother's reaction, It was before you were born, but I remember it as if it were yesterday. We had others before, of course but this one's all that's left. The others died a good while ago. A dog got one, I remember. This one's really old now," he said, stroking the grey whiskers around the chin of the huge tortoiseshell cat on his lap.

"Won't last forever. Just like me!"
The parents glanced at each other and then looked at Jane. She was staring at the bluebells.

As the others chatted during tea, she kept mostly quiet, and explained away the occassional tear as being because the flowers were not well, and the emotion of Molly giving birth was still fresh.

Soon after the tea had finished the old man began to show signs of tiredness, and at one point seemed to doze off. His son cleared away the trays, cleaned up, and put a blanket over him. They all said their goodbyes and promised to visit again the following weekend.

On their way home, the parents walked beside Jane and encouraged her to chat about how she was going to name Molly's other kittens. Philippa walked in front, turning round occassionally still desperate to hear all about what had happened. A look from her mother every time she was about to ask, stopped her.

Once home, they told Jane to check on her kittens, and the parents took the time to tell Philippa all she needed to know.

"That's amazing!" she said.

"Jane wasn't amazed, Phili," her mother replied. "It's a bit rough considering it's her birthday. So let's not say anymore about it to her."
Wishing she had been the one to witness it, Philippa shrugged, but didn't ask Jane about it till several days later.

"At least she has these kittens," she said.

After dinner, Jane got ready for bed, said goodnight to everyone and rushed up to her room carrying the basket with the cats inside. She tilted them out onto her bed and put the basket on the floor. Molly picked up each of her kittens and jumped off the bed and dropped them into her basket. She then climbed in and coiled round them as they fed. Jane lay face down on the bed and watched, and when the kittens seemed to have finished, she reached out and picked Milly up, and then leaned back and pulled the bedding over both of them. Hugging the kitten, she told her all about what had happened in the thicket, and wept on and off well into the night, till they both curled up and fell asleep.

The Compromise

The house was crooked. From the street all you could see was the high, creeper-clung wall and the splay of branches bragging clusters of bright, red berries. But after stooping through the heavy iron gateway and crossing the garden, you could see it was crooked. Eleven windows stared vacantly at the front garden, but only five were parallel to the flowerbeds below. Of the eleven rooms just four were now used, and only one had an occupant at any one time.

That occupant was now in a hammock hung between columns in the veranda. He had been there for three days. A stained, leather-topped table next to the hammock sustained an old notebook, a pencil stub, and a thick, dog-eared anthology of poems. Below it stood several empty bottles of red wine and a glass.

He was watching the moths circle the irresistible flames of a trio of candles, until they fizzled and fell into the warm, wax stalagmites at the base. He had counted them each night.

'...no time to stand and stare.'

For these three days he had been reading and drinking in search of inspiration. Some ideas, some phrases, seemed to arrive from somewhere above; light, banal and easily toyed with. Others seem to rise from the earth; dark, heavy and unwieldy. Neither had led him to anything that yielded more than insipid descriptions, and dead ends to chains of speculative thought that wouldn't adhere to the page for long. He was now feeling that he was being misguided, or worse, by his suroundings and the state he was in.

He pulled back the rough, woollen blanket and hung his legs over the side of the hammock. Balancing unsteadily on the edge, he felt the discomfort as blood flowed back to his thighs. He stood and shuffled to the bathroom, where he filled a large basin with cold water and slid his hands into it, cupping them beneath the surface and pulling them up to his lowered face, water cascading through his fingers. He repeated this action twice. The shock dispersed much of the mustiness from the past days. He placed his hands on the basin rim and straightened to look at the dripping face in the mirror. Strands of wet hair were stuck to the forehead, and the sunken, unshaven cheeks and the dark-rimmed eyes told of restless days and fitful sleep. He watched as a large droplet ran down the bridge of his nose and fell from the tip. Plunging his whole face into the deep basin, he scraped the top of his head against the taps. The lancinating pain opened his eyes and mouth wide, but he closed his throat to the scream and water, and kept his head under for as long as he could. When his will gave out, he pulled up and gasped. He felt the top of his head, his fingers returned streaked in watery red. Reaching for a hand towel, he dabbed his face and head until all water and blood stopped running. From the bathroom he went to an adjacent room, where he picked up a thick, knee-length overcoat and a handknitted woollen scarf. Clumsily pulling the former over his stale, rumpled clothes and wrapping the latter around the lower part of his face and neck, he went back to the verandah, picked up his things from the table, pushed them deep into the pockets, and left the house.

'I wish I could walk for a day and a night, and find me at dawn in a desolate place...'

Night had fully settled over the town. Streets were strips of darkness broken by lamp posts throwing thin skirts of light about themselves. As he walked, the buildings slowly emerged from the darkness ahead of him. Nearing the top of the hill at the edge of town, he looked back and saw the rooftops of the houses below in the thin moonlight. He imagined the tossing and turning, could almost see the miasma of unmet dreams and shackling fears rising above the sea of tiles.

'Are all the soul-and-body scars, too much to pay for birth?'

Feeling it was voyeuristic, he turned and walked on. Yellow lights in the windows of a large house at the top of the hill brought him to a stop. He watched as silhouettes moved slowly from one window to another, while others lurked behind the thin curtains. The house seemed to glow. He pushed on the gate and crossed the garden. At the porch, he stopped for a moment and listened. Voices of quiet authority were mixed with the inane questioning and defiance of the elderly who were in their care. He pulled down the brass lever of the door and, to the single chink of a small bell, entered. The smells hit him first. Then the clash of the furniture and décor, and finally the yellow-lit stillness. Everything gave the impression of an abandoned, amateur theatre set.

"Can I help you?" The bell had conjured someone from within.

"Oh…Are you all right?"

He stared at her until he remembered the face in the mirror.

'I am not cruel, just truthful.'

Very slowly, too slowly for her, he responded that he was. She watched him as he tried to get out more words. He backed away a little until his calves met the front of a sofa, and he sat down. He had no idea why he was there.

"Just need to sit a while," he heard himself say. She nodded slowly, half suspecting the devil was behind this visit.

"Do you have a relative here? It's not actually visiting hours, so maybe we could arrange something for tomorrow?"

He shook his head, and ran his hands through his hair in an attempt to fix his appearance. The pain as he touched the top of his head sharpened his thoughts, and the strength came to respond with a half lie.

"No, thank you. I've been ill, and foolishly I went out for a walk. I'm quite exhausted and I could find no other refuge. Do you mind? Just for a while."

Thoughts of the devil vanished, and she relaxed into her chatty, officious self.

"Of course. Would you like some water, or tea? I know that room 9 has just made a late pot. She wouldn't mind me borrowing a cup."

"Tea? No, no thank you. I'm fine, really."

'People measuring out their lives with teaspoons.'

'Room 9'. Even through his fog, that sounded cold.

"Well, if you're sure. I must be off on my rounds now. Please feel free to sit for a while. Get warm before you go home."

Her words were both advice and instruction.

Left to himself, he looked around the lobby. Photographs, crucifixes, and paintings of various saints donned the drab walls. One large oil hung over the sofa to his right. From it, almost obscene in its bulkiness, reared a huge, black bull with feathered banderillas sticking from its hump, and crimson streaks running down its thick neck and shoulders. Heavy dashes of paint gave the impression of the arena and the picadores surrounding the frantic, snorting beast. To one side of the painting stood an old, wooden lampstand with a frilly nylon shade that had faded blue cherubs floating round it. He stared at both. The bullfight scene, with its depiction of a life raging at death, palled in comparison. Nothing he had ever seen expressed more the approach of an abject finality than that lampshade.

The sister returned with an elderly woman clinging to her arm. They walked very slowly, the old woman never lifting her slippered feet off the green linoleum floor. As they passed in front of him, he could see the emptiness in the old woman's eyes, and hear her soft mewling.

"This is room 17," said the sister, as they shuffled passed.

"She's been here longer than anyone. Off to have a late supper, aren't we, my dear? We don't let her prepare anything in her room as she's gone rather gaga. Haven't you, my dear?"

The woman's nodding head was not an agreement.

"Are you feeling better now? Hello!"

It took a moment before he realised she was talking to him.

"Yes, yes, much. Thank you. I'll be off now. Thank you again."

"Right you are, dear. God bless."

He rose slowly, took one glance back at the lobby and left the home. He began walking along the road again. It was much colder, but it was a while before he realised he had left his scarf on the sofa. He would not go back now.

Reaching the foot of the far side of the hill, he turned off the road and onto a narrow lane. In a few minutes he was facing what once were dignified, wrought iron railings. Abandoned, their paint had peeled, their metal rusted. He pushed on the creaking gate and entered. A lone lamp post stood unlit near the centre of the cemetery. He sat on the bench beneath it and pulled his coat collar tighter around his neck. A waning moon threw pale light onto the headstones about him. The names cut into them he could not see, and would have recognised but few. Below them all reposed what the quick call 'death', the end to what the breathing call 'dying'. Beneath his feet they lay; seeping and gassy, dried and flaked, dismantled and crumbled.

After a while he took out his notebook and stub, and began composing.

'We are but a bloody hatch, then tepid compromise with Life, then…'

As he sat bent over the page, the cold air suddenly seemed to set about him, and it reached under his collar. He looked up. A tawny owl glided low out of the dark and alit on a headstone, its muffled call echoed from afar. Staring at the pale face, something thrilled within him, and he placed his notebook on the bench. His senses quickened to what he had been dead to while writing. Fireflies sparked at random above the grasses about him, as crickets chirped in rhyme below. The wind picked up and with it brought the scent of night jasmine. Cypresses soughed as they swayed, and tiny creatures rustled beyond the moonlight's sweep. His senses merged into a single point of awareness of the life abounding above the death below. He picked up his notebook and wrote for a good while longer.

Now feeling very cold, he rose, wrapped his coat about him and, clutching his things, he left. On his way home he passed the large house on the top of the hill. The lights were out; the raging and whimpering eternally deferred until morning. As he walked down the hill, he again saw the houses below. They were still, the dreaming within held tight beneath the waves.

Back in the veranda, he sat on the chair, opened his note book and slowly turned page after page of crossed out and half erased lines till he got to the pages he had written on in the graveyard. He read the lines over and over, until they seemed to have been written by someone else. Very slowly, very deliberately, he erased the few lines on the first page and underlined what was written on the rest. He closed the notebook and placed it with the anthology on the table. Wrapping the blanket over his coat, he curled himself into the hammock and closed his eyes. Behind them appeared images of the alabaster face and the tiny lights dancing around the graves, and the smell of jasmine filled his mind, like sound, as he fell deeply asleep.

Taking the Veil

It was after five, and the heat had become malicious. It clung, suffocating the air; it lay, scorching the streets; it hovered, causing the stained adobe houses to writhe.

The old woman carefully stepped down off the bus, rested her large, dusty bag on the hot stones and opened a parasol. She looked around her and drew two deep breaths. Picking up the bag, she slowly walked along the street. Soon, salty rivulets were running down her neck and under the collar of her black dress. Even below the parasol, the top of her head felt like summer hay. The bag, containing all she owned, clung damply to her side. The town was never crowded at this time of day; many were at home taking a siesta, some would be eating. None were doing what she was doing.

She came to a corner shop where candied fruits were melding into each other on a trestle table outside, and in which only the wasps seemed interested; an injudicious few trapped between the sheet of smudged, transparent plastic and the oozing, pulpy mounds. She put her things down and looked about her. The shop wall abutted that of the convent. Opposite, on the edge of the town plaza, stood an old donkey tethered under a large laurel tree. Beside it lay another, which the owner was trying to lift onto the back of a cart. Several men in bright ponchos came to help, and once the body was on the cart, the man untethered the donkey and, despite its stubborn resistance, managed to harness it to the shafts with fraying ropes. They then drew away and disappeared round the plaza.

In the store, she bought six cigarettes and six soft, toffee sweets. Outside again, she lit a cigarette and then picked up her things and walked on, keeping to the shade thrown by the stone wall of the convent. As she did, she could see the line of the top of the wall as it rose into the back of the cells, and then soared dramatically into the bell tower of the adjacent church. A minute later, she was at the cracked, wooden church doors. With one hand on the frame, she removed the cigarette, stubbed it out against the wall, and put it back into her bag with the other five.

Inside, it was dark, cool, and smelled of frankincense, wood polish and stone. Few pews were occupied, and she sat on an empty one near the front of the church facing the pulpit. Beside it, stood a plain wooden statue of St. Francis embracing a black lamb and leaning from the top of his stone column, as if searching for other lost sheep. Beyond this statue, close to the altar, stood a massive wooden one of a Christ with beckoning arms and a frown upon His forehead.

Dissonant pealing rang out from the bell tower. There were several minutes before mass would begin. As she gazed round the calm interior, she suddenly fully realized where she was, and felt the hope she had left home with in the morning renewed. The thin soles of her shoes gently rasped on the stone floor as she tried to settle into a more comfortable position on the unyielding wood. Reaching into her pocket, she took one of the sweets out of the bag and placed it in her mouth.

A large figure appeared from one side and made its way slowly from the sacristy, across the transept to the back of the altar. The priest's heavily bearded face looked out from atop the spotless white and purple vestment, whose gold ribbed folds could not hide the bulge of an indulged stomach. Most priests in the area were molded short, thin, dark, and clean shaven. His stoutness and black, slightly unkempt beard set against a large pale face seemed foreign, operatic even, yet comforting. The bells fell quiet as the mass was about to begin, and she discretely glimpsed behind her to see how many others had come. There was only a small group of elderly women all girded in blue and white checked aprons, a couple with four green-eyed, subdued children, and a dozen or so lone old men and women. Most of them had chosen to sit towards the back. Chords suddenly sounded out from the church organ. Looking up at the balcony, she could see the back of the organist's head in front of the pipes. She looked back to face the front of the church, where the priest had begun to open his sacramentary. The bell tower suddenly came to life again, and the organ and bells briefly competed in loud discord. The priest seemed unperturbed by the carelessness and waited; hands placed either side of the book.

Memories flooded in. Once, a lifetime ago, she had been in another country, another town, and in another church set in green Anglo-Saxon fields, dappled with sheep and contoured with dry-stone walls. She had always preferred the music over the words. There, the village church bells, resounding over meadow and vale, were seldom less than near sublime. There, the organ music was prayer in itself. Here, the bells were merely functional, a summoning in cracked bronze. Here, the organ was simply boon companion.

She sat following the mass, her gaze fixed on the figure of the priest. After the Gospel, the priest approached the pulpit. As he moved, she could see the large, white hands and heavily downed lower forearms beneath the cuffs of his garb. Hands and arms that she imagined led him daily along the white dirt tracks, through the dusty yards, scattering chickens and swine, and into the palm-thatched heart of his parish. The saint's petrified embrace seemed vitalized in the flesh and blood of such a man.

He stood in the pulpit and looked out over those sitting in the pews. The old woman could feel the haste of her pulsing heart. A flickering haze appeared at the edges of her sight. She became oblivious to all save the bulky presence in front of her. As the priest's first words began resounding through the church, she became aware of feeling slightly light-headed, and she knew that this momentary weakness was the effect of an understanding that seemed momentous, an understanding that whatever was to be said would be true. Whatever. His words would not fail. Feeling fainter, she leaned her chest and head over her thighs, put her elbows on her knees and rested her forehead on her closed hands. Her head spun as the undulant voice filled the nave. Suddenly, the vaulted ceiling swung to an impossible angle and seemed to pulsate. On the verge of complete darkness, she was aware of a tingling within her veins and a hardness beneath her, and she could hear muffled, overlapping voices. She felt strong arms lifting her up onto the pew, and she caught a strong smell of lotion. A concerned, authoritative voice was repeating something.

"It's alright, it's alright. You seem unhurt. You didn't really fall, more like slipped onto the floor, actually." His hands were on her shoulders. The realisation that the priest was speaking to her in English impelled her to her senses. A weak smile broke over her wan face, and she replied thickly, "No, no. I'm fine, really. Thank you very much."
The proximity of the priest was all she needed.

"Alguien le puede traer agua, por favor?" he said to those standing round.

"Just sit here for a minute and we'll fetch you some water. Quite a scare, but it's probably just the heat."

"Yes…yes, I think so…Thank you."

There was no need for fuss. The consuming sense of urgency that had been haunting her was now seen for what it was, and it was vanishing. It would be almost silly to mention it. She focused on the priest as he engaged in conversation with two of the apron-clad women who had gathered round them. The man was so solid, so real…so right. And somehow he had known where she was from. She felt a tremendous relief and a thrill of anticipation.

Helped up by one of the women, she stood and drank some of the water she was offered. Then, giving an unsmiling, but grateful look into the priest's delving eyes, she bowed her head to the others about her and picked up her belongings. Hugging them, she carefully made her way down the aisle, silently accompanied by the priest, to the portal, where he bade her farewell. Out on the street, she stood in the shade of a younger kin of the laurel in the plaza and smoked the rest of the cigarette. She then picked out another of the sweets from the bag, and let it melt in her mouth as she made her way back along the street that led her to the convent door.

The Gardener and the Prior

That morning the Gardener and the Prior woke at the same time but having had very different dreams, and both lay a while thinking quite dissimilar thoughts, until distant crowing announced the hour.

As the cold light outside began to outline the world in pre-dawn greys, the Prior pulled aside his clean, neatly-mended, woollen blankets and rose from his bed, only to ease to his heavy knees in prayer. On the other side of the monastery, the Gardener threw off his blankets and set his legs over the edge of his low wooden bed and fed his thin, leathery feet into broken sandals before offering up his own. He knelt for a short while longer, trying to dispel the wisp-like remnants of his dream. Moments later, they both left their rooms, and drawn by the pealing from the belfry, made their ways to the church for the second prayer service of the morning.

The Prior's path lay around the east side of the cloister and in through a side door of the stone-ribbed nave. The Gardener's was circuitous, but much more worn; out through the heavy oak doors that gave to the several lay dormitories, down each of the seventeen mildewed, concave stone steps, and round the north side of the cloister, to join growing tributaries of other monks silently coursing round the columns and along the passages, and eventually into the church. The stream of monks flowed into the banks of pews and, once there, a great stillness settled, and in common obeisance, the group of one hundred and seventy black hooded figures spent the next half-hour deep in prayer, silent and still, except for the occasional impassioned murmurs and gentle swaying of the more ancient and less worldly souls.

The monastery had been there long before any of them had entered under their different imperative callings. Like numerous other monasteries in the land, it had provided its own alloy of fellowship and solitude, or escape and deliverance, for all types of men and, save for the fires of reform or whims of monarch, it would go on doing so for long after even the youngest of these one hundred and seventy had been lain, arms folded upon his inert chest, beneath the clammy earth.

The whole complex was dominated by the two things that had guided the inceptive gothic inspiration: the massive church that loomed over the whole area to the north, and the small, cheerful river that slid round and under many of the buildings in the south. Between them the fragrant cloister reposed, surrounded above ground by the sonorous dormitories, two kitchen gardens, cavernous refectory, and replete library and scriptorium, and below ground by the buttery and cellarum, the calefactory and one dank prison cell. Scattered amongst all these and at various heights stood the pentagonal chapter house, the grand Abbot's house, the infirmary with its lone, moribund patient, the silent locutory, foul latrines, heady brew house and vast, vaporous kitchen. Off to the east, lay the crenellate cemetery, sinister, green fish ponds, empty stables, and across the river to the south lay three weedful gardens, the chicken coops, overgrown sheep pens and miry sties, and the tall barns. Further still were the meadows and deciduous woods.

Almost as one, the heads and backs straightened, and the tide of robes, including those of the Prior and Gardener, ebbed away into the halls and back to its variegated source.

The Gardener's room lay to one side of the calefactory, and was graced with an unusually generous window at one end, which allowed for a clear view of the extensive kitchen gardens. This gave his mind great peace, for he was far more in keeping with seasonal and diurnal rhythms than any of his brothers.

He did not stay long in his room. After refreshing his face and hands in ice cold water, he pulled on a moth-eaten, mud-stained woollen cloak, closed his door behind him, and descended the stairs. He left the building through a low back door that gave onto a path which took him to that part of the monastery he called his true earthly home. For over three decades he had adored and tended his gardens and livestock.

Here, there was only one higher Being, and like Him, here, the Gardener beheld all, from root-deep seasonal changes to the tiniest blemish of contagion on the underside of a green leaf.

The garden and the Gardener were one. In the herber together they grew cloves for toothache, witch hazel for haemorrhoids, chamomile for indigestion, cardamon for flatulence, parsley for lice, and thyme for melancholy. In the kitchen garden they grew red beet and yellow bean, orange carrot and purple onion, white porrette and worts of varying green. In the sties and pens and coops beyond grunted, bleat and clucked the other members of his bucolic family.

But the monastery was not as it once had been. Only a decade ago it had been one of the three most prosperous monasteries in the north. Over five hundred monks lived there, the wool trade was booming and the monastery grew corpulent and slothful, and was dazzled by its own golden light. But a terribly misunderstood, invisible enemy had swiftly crippled much of the land, and its incursion into the church, dormitories and infirmary had brought the monastery to its knees in supplication. As the monastery life waned, so had the extent of his labour been pared. Fewer mouths to feed had naturally led to large uncultivated patches of stony earth, drier pig pens, and more lamb that grew to mutton.

As he bent down to remove a small flint shard from the heart of a young cabbage, he thought of the purpose of the Abbott's apparently successful quest and his arrival tomorrow, and again felt the despair that had given rise to his earlier dream.

The Prior had also gone back to his chambers after leaving the church. As he opened the door to his large ante-room and ducked under the ornate stone lintel, he recalled the dream that he had had earlier. A sudden light-headedness came over him and he sat on the end of the soft bed. A momentary thrill sharpened his blood and he forced himself to focus on his upcoming chores to keep from releasing an unseemly giggle into the room. His day would normally be spent in both the smaller and greater aspects of running the monastery, but this day would be dedicated to getting the monastery as well prepared as possible. The Abbot and his entourage had been away for nearly three months and they were due back the next day. Suppressing a second surge of felicity with a self-conscious cough, he stood up and tenderly washed his sagging, slightly seedy face and fat, prim hands in the beautiful, chipped, Sicilian ceramic basin below the window. As he gently dabbed his skin with a soft woollen towel, he raised his head and looked out of the window. He could see the Gardener bent over in the garden picking something out of a plant.

He put on a clean robe, left the room and went to the chapter house. There he saw several of the monks engaged in quotidian administrative work and a few organising the welcome for the Abbot. As he passed by their tables, he met their inquiring glances with encouraging nods and smiles. Reassured by his presence and apparent good humour, some settled deeper into their tasks, but others approached him with an increased sense of camaraderie.

"Brother David, is it true what is being said?" said one.

"And what exactly is being said, brother Francis?" asked the Prior, with a hint of condescension in his voice.

"They say the Abbot has it with him as he travels. They say it is miraculously well preserved. They say he was given it in a locked, silver box and that there is only one key, and that no one has opened it yet."

"Indeed! Well, they seem to be saying too much…and too little, I fear," replied the Prior. There were several more attempts to get him to confirm as true other choice hearsay, but he hurried out of the large room after telling all concerned to be patient and pray for the Abbot's safe return. He knew more of the truth than them, and much less of the gossip. He knew the Abbot had been successful in his quest, and he believed that now the monastery would be restored to its former glory. He had been praying most fervently for that for a long time.

As he hurried down the hall towards the stairs, he pushed one hand deep into the inner side of his robe until he reached a concealed pocket from which he removed an exquisite, enamelled flask with the bust of a cherub in gold leaf on the front, and a white pearl half-embedded in the top of the gold stopper. Pausing briefly so as not to spill any, he took three deep draughts of the sweet, potent mead. From another pocket he took out a small lozenge made from the oils of mint and violet petals and crunched on it noisily as he climbed the stairs to the scriptorium.

His entrance to this room was all but ignored by the six wizened monks who were engrossed in copying the curled manuscripts and garnishing the sagacious texts. These monks were of greater age than even the Abbot and had entered before him, and their lives were dedicated to copying and preserving the Gospels and Hellenistic wisdom. However, senility and decades of routine had long ago dulled their appreciation of the content of what they copied, and the finely crafted initial letters and marginal embellishment were now for them of far greater import than the meanings so adorned. It was this Noachian sextet that had been instrumental in engineering the monks' vote to raise the capable brother Albert to the exalted position of Abbot. They had been indifferent to brother David's own promotion to Prior some years later. Despite what time had done to them, he was occasionally uneasy in their presence, but his mood today, carried over almost into glee by the thick wine, took his strides to their very table top. He stood in front of them. They looked shrunken and stupid. He stifled a giggle, and placed his palms flat down on the surface of the table and addressed the top of their bald heads.

"Brothers, you will soon have new manuscripts to work on. Your, our glory is returning with what the Abbot brings tomorrow."

The monks slowly turned to each other.

"I heard 'tis a golden bag containing part of Saint Jerome's dream," shrilled one.

"No," said another, an octave higher. "It is, I have been assured, his Hebrew grammar."

"I hear 'tis two of Saint Audrey's necklaces," wheezed a third.

"I overheard the Abbot saying he was going to Paris to get the hands of Saint Denis," boomed a fourth.

"Not at all!" brayed another. "'Tis the first chant ever penned by Saint Ambrose. The Abbot told me himself in confidence."

But it was only to the Prior that the Abbot had mentioned the true purpose of his journey to the continent and his sojourn in Tours and Paris, and the Abbot had made him vow not to mention it. He straightened, and lifted his hands from the wooden surface. A sigh escaped his thick nostrils, as his mind filled with an image from his dream. An image, as if through a thin sheet of ice, of a beehive oozing honey which, while dreaming it, had thrilled him.

He looked at the six ovine faces, all of which had already gone back to their set positions and expressions in front of rolls of parchment and tomes of half-finished copies of sacred texts ten times as ancient as themselves, and ten thousand times as wise. He left the room and descended the stairs. The Abbot's was an aged, unwieldy body and not used to such incommoding trips as the one he had taken this time. It was necessary to check there would be enough turnip and piglet for the Abbot's favourite pottage, and enough sweet mead to ensure a tight, holy sleep.

By the time he arrived at the low dry-stone wall beside which the Gardener was working, the Gardener had been happy for nearly an hour. So absorbed was he by the task at hand, he was quite unaware of the multitude of larger contexts for his present acts, and his mind, being free of doubt, was quite empty of the many thoughts that can arise in the speculative minds of those to whom such manual labour is pleasant but not customary. Thoughts such as, could the beauty of the flowers about the garden beguile Him. Such as, perhaps the Almighty knows us not and thus religous rapture is merely the precipitate of defeated self-love.

As he deftly danced the iron blade between the tender green stems and sundered and sequestered the unwanted growth from the damp clods, his mind was only filled with the immediacies of the freshly turned soil before him and the verdure about him. But the sudden sight of the incongruous, massy body intruding upon his garden tightened his stomach, and he straightened. From over the wall, he watched the white puffs of vapour as the Prior exhaled heavily into the world, and through the earthy musk he could smell the flowery, fermented breath.

The Prior beheld the thin, purposeful frame with the sleeves of its cloak rolled back from the elbows, and the soiled feet. Even the warmth from the mead could not thaw his tone.

"Prithee, brother, how fares Canaan?"

"All is well, brother," the Gardener replied.

"Good! Much will be needed for tomorrow's festivities. We once made Rome herself proud, and with what the Abbot brings hither we shall do so again. Pilgrims will flock here again. Then you will be properly busy. Our dormitories and fields will be filled again."

"And the coffers," replied the Gardener.

"You verge on sacrilege, brother," the Prior replied.

"The blight wasn't sent by the Lord for want of relics," said the Gardener. "It left fallow many an acre and dry many a pen, yes, but other things were left fallow before. 'Tis shameful you know this not!"

The Prior swept one short, heavy arm round in a semicircle.

"This is not the daily bread of our prayers. Greater fare is needed to sate other glorious hungers. That is what I know."

He caught himself. The effects of the mead had disappeared like his own breath in front of him. He looked steadily at the figure in front.

"I came hither not to dispute such matters. I came to see there would be enough for the Abbot's favourite supper tomorrow."

"Enough, and more than, as always."

The Prior took one step back, and for several seconds they stood on opposite sides of the wall like two statues, until the Prior was startled by the ringing from the belfry announcing the next prayer meeting. For a long moment the peals seemed to hang over the garden.

Slightly embarrassed at having shown the start the bells had given him, the Prior dropped his eyes and stepped carefully onto the path, and without looking back, he made his way to the church. The Gardener watched the tightly robed rolls on his back for a few moments, and once the Prior had turned from sight, breathed deeply, and with the cold economy of movement his anger had given him, he leaned the wooden shaft of his hoe against the wall opposite the exact place in the furrow where the earth was still unturned, and followed.

Indistinguishable now among the last wave of hoods, the two monks found the front pews full, and from opposing sides of the nave made their separate ways to the half empty rows near the back. In the caesura between the thrum and drone of the first two prayers, the Gardener raised his head only to see the same tightly-clothed, fleshy back a few rows in front of him. But he gazed at it as if it were of a complete stranger as his prayers gained strength, and he abandoned himself to the Godhead.

When the prayers ended, the rest of the monks left leaving the Gardener and the Prior lingering, their minds now occupied by the residue of their individual dreams.

Turtle Dreams

"Next question," said Lily.

"Hang on. Hang on. Ok…what's redder than red?" Tom said.

"Er…Ha! It's crimson! Easy!"

"Ok, ok. Good one, but you had to think tons!" he replied. "Your turn."

"My turn…hmmm…what's the biggest fruit in the whole wide world?"

"Oh…er…ah, yeah! It's…"

The twins, Lily and Tom, were sat round Stumpy, the mossy remains of a long-dead oak tree at the bottom of their garden. It was their secret place, and even though everyone else in the family and the neighbours across the way knew about it, and could see them when they were there, it was their secret place.

Twins they were and would always be, but Lily was seven minutes older than Tom, (that made her nine years, two months, thirteen days, eight hours, twenty nine minutes, forty two seconds old, when she said 'crimson').

Those extra seven minutes were something she was proud of, and she made sure to mention it whenever needed.

"It's a watermelon!" said Tom. "Ha! I'm winning!"

"Wrong! It's a pumpkin! So we're tied and it's my turn again."

Tom readied himself for a really tough question.

"Does Percy dream?" she said.

"Hey!" said Tom. "That's a big question! You're cheating, I'm not a turtle!"

"Dogs dream, don't they," said Lily, undeterred.

"Look! Rufus is moving his legs!" she had once commented. "Like he's running."

"He's just dreaming," her father had said. "Like when you saw Percy lying on the stones at the bottom of the tank. You thought he was dead, but he was asleep, and maybe dreaming too."

"I remember," said Tom. "And mother says everyone dreams every night."

Lily paused a while.

"So if we dream when we're asleep," she said, "and dogs do too, maybe turtles do when they sleep. Maybe they have scary dreams sometimes. But we usually forget our dreams. Do you think they forget them, too?"

"I hope not," said Tom, "because the ones I remember are fun, well most of them are. I still remember the one I had about you as a flying hedgehog bursting all my party balloons. I was so angry with you for days after that! And you looked so stupid!"

"Haha, I bet! said Lily. And then in a different tone, "But I'm sorry I did that."
They looked at each other, both feeling the apology didn't make sense, but neither was quite sure why. The game now forgotten, they sat chatting about dreams till they heard their mother calling them in for supper.

Later that night, after their parents had read them a story, kissed them and turned off the lights in their room, they lay silently in their beds looking up into the dark wondering what dreams they would have, and Lily fell asleep wondering whether Percy would have some too.

Tom's dream was one he never, ever forgot. He was running as fast as he could down the garden and, before he reached Stumpy, he pushed himself upwards and began to soar above the garden and out over the street. He could see Lily way below waving at him. Thrilled at being so high up, he began to dive and soar like a kite in the breeze, each time gaining more and more control over his movements. It was the most amazing dream possible.

Lily's dream was very different; she dreamed about dreams. She dreamed of a voice that spoke to her.

"We are your dreams, Lily, and we come from your heart and mind, and beyond. And we know you. During the busy, sunlit day you work and play at home and school, but once the sun has set and your eyes are closed tight, we visit you. We visit you, everyone you know and every other living thing: your sister, your parents, your friends, your neighbours, your turtle, every ladybird and elephant, every eagle

and whale, every tree and buttercup. One or two of us have even been visited ourselves.

We tell stories that only the sleeping can hear. Stories where things are never as they seem. In our stories, ice is never cold, winds never blow, rain never wets, and fire never burns, so our dragons couldn't even melt an ice cream. In them, nothing is born and nothing dies, yet everything lives.

Our stories are like the stories your parents read to you. Ours disappear in the opening of an eye, just as the stories you read disappear in the closing of the book. But when the book is closed, does the story really end? Don't you sometimes think about it, or talk about it to friends and family. Don't you even ask your parents to read it again? With us, when you open your eyes our stories end. But do they really end? You sometimes remember them for a long while after, and some you even remember for the rest of your life! And now and then, if needed, we might tell you the same story again.

The stories your parents read to you contain messages, but the stories don't tell you what their messages are, you have to think and explore that yourself. Our stories are like that, we don't tell you what they mean. We want you to explore what the messages might be. That can be great fun.

That's what we do. We send you messages. Sometimes our stories are not very good, and they are forgotten easily, but sometimes they are so good we even surprise ourselves, and those stories are never forgotten. As I said, we know you well, even better than you might think, and all our stories just try to help you see things more clearly when you later awake, things that we see more clearly when you are asleep.

I hope you will remember all this when you wake, Lily. After all is said and done, we dreams should know a thing or two about dreaming."

She woke up soon after the dream finished, and lay in bed thinking. This was a dream like no other, and she felt it was very important and she had to share it with Tom as soon as possible.

She sat up and saw his eyes were open. He was lying in bed remembering how good it felt to fly. Before she could say anything he bubbled over with his description of it.

"I had a dream where I was flying! It was amazing! I ran so fast and I could take off and land and swoop up and down and I didn't even have to flap! I saw all the houses and our garden and street and you were waving to me from way below and…oh…it was so much fun! I was like a bird!"

He caught his breath and sat up.

"Did you dream?"

Lily got up and sat on the edge of his bed.

"Yeah, I had a dream too, but mine was very weird. My dream told me about dreams."

"What? You had a dream about dreams? Wow! Tell!"

She told him all about it.

"So he does dream! You were right!" he exclaimed.

Their mother's voice rose from the kitchen calling them to breakfast.

"Let's go," said Tom. "We must tell them."

Tom was first, and he described everything he could remember between mouthfuls of toast and marmalade.

"Was that your first dream of flying?" his mother asked.

"Yes, yes it was. I really hope I have more," said Tom. The parents looked at each other and smiled.

Lily didn't forget anything when she described hers. She also remembered the dream for the rest of her life. Both parents looked long at her after she finished.

"Your dream was very special, Lily, very…very magical," her mother said.

Intrigued by the dreams, especially Lily's, the parents spent the rest of the breakfast exploring what the children thought about their dreams.

From that day on, every time the twins sat down with Stumpy to share their dreams, they took great guesses as to what the dreams were saying. And the next time they went for an ice cream they looked at each other, and then held their ice creams aloft, daring any dragon to come and melt them. The ice creams did melt, of course, but they knew why and laughed as they imitated dragons' breath while nibbling on them.

Percy's dream was forgotten as soon as it finished, but it was about him resting on a smooth, mossy stepping stone, and feeling the warm sun on his back as he dipped his feet in the cool, rippling waters, before sliding in and slowly swimming over an endless, stoney, river bed.

Window on the Week

"Morning, Sue. Got a moment to spare? I need some input on a little conundrum. How do you parse *what's he do*, you know, as in '*what's he do for a living*'?" It was only 7:22 and there were still eight minutes before the first class.

Susan Conim, the high school Literature and Creative Writing teacher, smiled as she opened the door for him. Married to her work, poetry and late quartets, nearing retirement and thinning on top, she considered herself a friend and ally to all in the school, and was adored by her students.

Brian Nets was the teacher who, upon meeting Sue outside the staff room, had started the weekly banter. Nets was the Sports and Phys. Ed. teacher, and he and two other junior members of the faculty had shaken hands on a covenant at the end of the half term break that demanded they asked her about apparent linguistic anomalies, with which, under the guise of genuine inquiry, they tried to challenge her. She was sightly bemused at first, and, if truth be told, also a little proud that these younger staff members had recourse to her in order to resolve such riddles.

"Well, I think that might not prove as challenging as a question posed to me only last week by George," she replied.

That one, posed by George Lewgh, the Philosophy teacher, had been whether the greater value of a noun was to be found in its denotation, or in the sum of its connotations.

"So, what do you think, Sue?" Nets urged, as he edged through the door hugging his briefcase, files, clipboard and football against his chest.

"Allow me a short mulling and you'll have it by end of day. All right?" She closed the door behind him and left for the reception area.

After dumping his things on the sofa, he headed straight to the coffee maker and poured himself a mug full. As he went to sit next to his pile of paper and leather, two other colleagues entered and greeted him.

"Tarp o' da marnin tooya," Irished Alan Tunrig, the Computer Science teacher. Reasonably good at copying regional accents, and very good at copying software, he was very popular with his peers.

"Chilly, what?" he R.P'ed. And it was. The end of February and no end to the morning frosts and icy evening winds in sight. Tunrig went to the machine, and grinning, returned and sat next to Nets, even though twenty other seats were available.

"Think I've got her this time," whispered Nets. Tunrig, like most colleagues, knew about the 'covenant', but was slightly taken aback by the harshness in Net's tone.

The other colleague to enter was the veteran teacher Charles Ardwin, 'Chuck' to his buddies, as he called all and sundry. His was the challenge of inculcating into the students an appreciation of matters floral and faunal. He had a penchant for devising imaginative hands-on lab work which often led to squeals of disgust and oohs of coy interest and, more felicitously, instilling a real attraction in the students to the biota of their own environs. His new addition to the school gardens, a large, walled plant-bed in the shape of the country with many of the main regional plants growing in their respective zones, was much admired by all.

He looked up at the clock. "What time d'y'all have?"

"My watch says 7:29:55, so…all together…4,3,2…". And the bell rang for the next class.

"Oh, she's sor gud is ouwa Sue," Welshed Tunrig. Ardwin nodded as he set the wall clock to the right time.

II

Lilian Quint, the venerable, late middle-aged headmistress, closed her thick, leather-bound diary and placed her thick, expensive pen upon it. According to that book and her clock, it was time for her daily walk around the school. Irish, well-educated and as maternal as any headmistress should be, she also had a dry streak, which in many a thin person might have been rather unpleasant, but in her well-dressed, ponderous frame it achieved the status of an enjoyable, sometimes delicious, quirk. It most commonly expressed itself in barbs designed to deflate the more self-satisfied or lax members of her team.

She left her dark, wooden-panelled office and, picking up her metal clipboard, shuffled her sharp, cultivated mind and blunt, neglected body forth into the light of day.

Physically, the school was a mixture of new, inoffensive, imitation colonial buildings and older, decidedly offensive mid-20th century constructions. There were well-kept flower beds between each block and large areas of sports fields near the road. The design of these newer classrooms was, as rumour had it, partly inspired by the ease with which she could evaluate the classes within from without. During her walks she could often be seen lingering outside the small one-way glass window at the end of each room and listening, witnessing what she quaintly called 'jam sessions', rather than the over-rehearsed 'studio recordings' of programmed observations.

Always completely cognisant of which teacher should be where and when before even the second week of term was over, she stopped by the window of the High School seniors' room B, through which she could see Lewgh at his desk and a student in front of the board. From that same vantage point, she could also just hear the voices within.

One of the best students was in front holding the attention of the group with an obviously competent speech on whether the intentions or effects of a person's actions were of greater importance when assessing that person's moral compass. Lewgh, chin cupped in his hands, was listening intently. The student finished to appreciative applause. Lewgh released his head and turned to the class.

"Excellent! Ok. Let's see...who has some questions for Andrea? Remember, what is it that encourages thought?"

"Tons of good questions," several students shouted out.

"And what is it that's kills thought?" he asked.

"Too many of these things," came the reply.

"Exactly!" A smile creased the sides of his mouth.

Andrea handled the questions well, looking each questioner in the eyes and without once looking at Lewgh.

"Ok...so now finally, Beto, please recap for us all what Andrea's position on this topic is."

Beto recapitulated well.

"Very good! Everyone took notes? All right. Well done again, Andrea and Beto."

He gently joined in the applause.

"Now I want to invite...Bob."

Roberto, the last student to perform the task, stood up and strutted to the front, giving a few high-five's as he came down between the rows. At the front, he rocked to-and-fro a while, turned 360 degrees twice, and then embarked on two false starts. Suddenly, he began to mumble a series of platitudes on his topic of the 'death penalty'. He stopped well before the denouement, and to thunderous applause, whistles and feet stomping, he bowed and pumped his fist in the air. Grinning, he turned to the teacher.

Lewgh's whole face was cupped in his hands; it had been since the student's first pirouette. A second later his head rose rather rapidly. He blinked three times.

"Okay...now who wants to summarise this one?" As she walked away to the next classroom, Lilian jotted down a few notes on what she had seen, and a mental note of the barb she would let fly.

III

It was the long morning recess, and many of the teachers were in the lounge. Had the flies on the wall above the machine been students, they would have seen most of the teachers' mouths at work: some munching on the best choice from yesterday's tray of biscuits; a few of them still, albeit sotto voce, conversing with the last class, improving on what they had actually said; and several others stretched wide in yawns.

Around the outer edges of the room were arrayed many of the teachers' desks, each with its idiosyncratic display of devices, decorations and dross. The surfaces of the small white boards above most of the desks were barely visible beneath a multicoloured patchwork of sticky notes from students and colleagues The most densely covered was that of the students' favourite teacher. The second most densely covered was that of a teacher who, it was maliciously averred, penned most of them himself.

This was the time for further banter with Sue.

"Sue, my love!" bellowed Sleat, the junior science teacher. "How come 'inert' exists, but not 'ert'?"

"And what about increasing?" hollered Nets.

They all looked at him.

"What about it, my petal?" said Sleat.

"Why doesn't 'increasing' mean creasing in, when 'ingrowing' means growing in?"

Several pairs of eyebrows were raised, and there was even one sharp laugh, belatedly disguised as a cough, though from whom was not clear.

"Seems you are both very much awake to the little quirks of our wonderful language," she said, meeting Nets' gaze. Ardwin had his back to most of them, as he was pouring a coffee, but a wry grin had parted his moustache from his beard.

"Ignore them, Sue," he said. "Who was it said Man's ignorance can be useful and even beautiful? One of our Transcendentalists, I believe." Turning, he faced the others "We have here a clear case of just how wrong he could be."

There was a silence while the rest took in this unexpected assault.

"Ardwin, I'm not sure, but I have the feeling you have just likened Nets to a nescient, ineffectual, gargoyle," said Lewgh.

Nets had understood little of their gibes, but looked at Sleat, grinning sheepishly. Lewgh was looking steadily at Sue.

Saved by the bell.

IV

" …but how, Sue? Look, in my poem I'm in some wood at night and I can see moonlight on a mossy rock. I'm trying to describe that, but I can't. It's like…flat, you know? Reading what I wrote doesn't get close to making me feel what it would be like to actually be there."

"Then you should paint it," said another student. Anne looked at him and silently fiddled with the notebook on her desk.

"Mm… OK. That's an interesting point, Philip," Sue replied. "Written words, like in a poem, are visible, like scenes in a painting are, but they are not only visible, we can also hear them, and that matters just as much, I think. But when we're experiencing poems, I mean writing or reading them, often the experience simply involves seeing the written words, the series of marks on a paper, and thinking about the meanings. Much as we might experience a painting, looking at the marks on the canvas, say. That is, at least, the main part of the experience for many people. We must do that, of course, but then we should go beyond the written words, the visible words. The sounds of the words and phrases in a poem can evoke even more than the mere sight of them. Seeing the words in a poem, in other words reading silently, is common, it's the norm, and the words can lose much power as a result. And therefore, so can their poems. Great poets don't just read their lines, their poems, they read them aloud. The best poets are tuned in to the sounds of the words and phrases they use. They try to match the sounds of the individual words, or of the groups of soft or hard sounds, and of the rhythms of the lines, to the content of the poem. Remember, we've seen some basic metrical patterns and things like onomatopoeia. But why stop there? Everything described in the poem we've been reading was something Wordsworth saw. I mean, he looked at the flowers and lake and clouds, but surely he must have also heard things, smelled things, or even picked a flower. He doesn't talk about that, unfortunately. It seems it wasn't part of the experience for him. He didn't, but he could have immersed himself into the experience with all his senses, and incorporated that into the poem. Then the recollection would have been even richer. For example, what could he have heard?"

"The wind."

"His footsteps."

"Smell?"

"The flowers."

"His sweaty body."

Laughter.

"Yes, Roberto, yes, very probably, as he had been walking. What else?"

"The water from the lake."

"What could he feel?"

"The water too, right? Maybe he put his hand in the water."

"Good, good," said Sue. "My point is that we should use as many senses as we can in such experiences, and when experiencing poems, as a writer or reader, we should do the same. We should plunge in with all we've got and squeeze the most out of the language as we can."

"Isn't that a mixed metaphor, Sue?" a student asked.

Laughter.

"It most certainly is. Well spotted, Frankie," she said, smiling.

"Aren't you really saying that that we should 'plunge in' as you call it, into all our experiences, like life, or just with poetry and stuff?" said Anne.

Sue looked long at her.

"Lovely question, Anne. Explore that in your journal and I'd love to read it. It would be a great journal topic for all of you. By the way, did you know that apparently in some non-literate societies, people try to duck out of the way of swear words spoken to them? They literally duck when they hear the swear words, as if they were stones. Those sounds, those words have power!"

"Like which, Sue?"

"Nice try, Roberto."

When the laughter and clapping died down, Sue continued.

"You see, Anne, it's not the marks you can see on the paper. It's ironic, I know, but they're distracting you. Writing that poem you mentioned, first use your imagination and dive into the scene with as many senses as you can, and then listen to what you use to describe what the whole experience of being there would be. Then the reading aloud of the poem will have more chance to convey the richness of the actual experience for the reader."

Anne looked at her. "That's what I want to happen, exactly that."

"You want your readers to feel that when they read your poem, but first you must feel that when you write it," Sue said.

Even before Sue finished her last point, Anne had begun erasing and crossing out what now seemed wrong. Most of the others followed suit very soon. Sue opened her notebook and, pushing aside her class planner, began to write a few lines down too.

V

The secretary popped her head round the door of the teachers' lounge and greeted all present.

"George, Lilian was wondering if you could pop by today, sometime after the first break."

Not surprised, he mustered up the will to respond. A nod was all he managed, the image of Roberto in his mind.

"George is here," she said.

"Thanks, Mary. Please show him in."

He entered and was greeted warmly. Sitting opposite her at her desk, he leaned back in the chair and folded his arms, then quickly unfolded them. He brought them to rest at his side, palms on his thighs.

"Good of you to come, George. Here, have a chocolate." She proffered her box of dark chocolates and George deftly removed one. Not sure whether he should eat it now or later, he decided to keep it between the thumb and index finger of his right hand. Her phone rang and she answered quickly. Taking the opportunity to nibble on the softening sweet while she spoke, he noticed his finger and thumb were smeared in chocolate. Deciding wisely not to lick them, he hid his hand under the table.

"Sorry about that," she said, "but back to what I wanted to chat about. I had the pleasure of listening in on your class on Monday…the one on ethics with the seniors…remember?"

He did, but his current predicament was overriding everything, causing a strangled chuckle to escape his lips.

"Are you OK?"

He chuckled again, and held up his hand.

"Goodness! How silly of me. Here, have some tissues. How embarrassing! I just didn't think. Here we are, on the verge of discussing your class, and the indignities suffered by one of our colleagues and a student of yours, and I've let a little chocolate get the better of us," she said.

They looked at each other as he cleaned the last of the stains from his thumb. The incongruity of it all made her smile.

"Can I be frank?" he said, leaning over and placing the tissues in the waste bin by the desk.

"Always, please."

"I think you know but…I respect you, very much, but I have never really felt we clicked. That is until now." He followed his candour with a smile. It lit up his normally dour face.

"Truly, George, I am glad," she said. She no longer felt the need of the barb she had prepared.

"Your class was very good. I especially like your focus on higher thinking skills, and proactive listening, However, there is one matter I wish to go into in more detail, though I am sure you are, at heart, fully in agreement with me."

"Roberto, right?"

"Yes, Roberto."

"Roberto's not a bad kid, at all," he said. "But he's a terrible student, and he shouldn't be here. He drags down every serious work we do to an inane level. Not fair on the others, or me."

"I understand, George. But the point is, he is here, and until he leaves, for whatever reason, he must be treated with respect, and more, given real encouragement. I know all your other students get at least that from you, but I need you to feel and act in accordance with that premise in his case."

He did agree and act accordingly in general, and this one exception proved it. He nodded.

She said no more about it.

"As we have got off to such a great start today, let me be frank, if I may," she said.

Most teachers faced with such a comment would have fidgeted a little in their chair and straightened up. Rarely on the defensive, but never defenceless, he just looked into her eyes enquiringly. She had mentioned two indignities.

"I know about the game, so to speak, that some of the younger staff are playing with Susan. As far as I have ascertained, it seems fairly innocent. I need to know if it really is. I'm asking you because I heard you've occasionally joined in, something, which I must admit, surprises me."

He explained how the one time he had asked her a question she took it like that, but he had genuinely wanted her input.

"Maybe she's getting too trapped in it," he said. "I've been there when they tease. It's a bit of harmless fun."

"Always?"

"Well, no, not always in intent with one of them, but she doesn't seem to notice. Or maybe she's too good a 'sport'. Australians use that word a lot, right? 'Sport.'" They looked at each other steadily.

As he was leaving, she offered him two more chocolates. She closed the door behind him, returned to her desk and sat in thought. On his way back to his room, Lewgh popped both chocolates into his mouth and licked his fingers.

VI

Near the end of his twenty-minute ride to school the next day, Lewgh could see the pleasing terra cotta roofs and white walls of the older school buildings, and the brick-red arch over the main entrance. From the car park, he made his way through the grounds towards the senior school buildings. Passing the lower grades schoolyard, he heard the squeals of the very young in earnest play, and he lingered a while to watch. He was well aware of the parents' meeting mantra that 'kids are the future', but after years in front of chalk and then whiteboard, he could only feel the truth of that in their company. In the company of most adults, especially his colleagues, he could only ponder the naivety of those who, generations ago, chanted it. A believer in the liberating power of irony and paradox in general, this was one paradox he felt he should be able, but forever feared, to explain away.

He continued on until the sights and sounds of the children were replaced by the voices and the purposeful movements of staff members as they passed him on their ways to and fro. All tendered friendly smiles and brief words of greeting, though knowing full well he seldom returned more than a candid look in their eyes and a nod. Only the deaf gardener, who always took the time to look up from his tasks and beam a wrinkled, holy smile at him, received more.

Nearing the door to the building he saw one of his students, Sally, sitting on a bench alongside another student who was helping her to put her books back into her satchel. Upon seeing him approach, the child lifted her pale, gaunt face and an emaciated arm and moved her hand in a slow waving motion. At the bench, Lewgh half knelt beside her and cupped her hand in both of his and quietly spoke to her. There was a look about her, a look in her eyes which he knew would always haunt him. The other girl, still hugging the satchel, watched him as he spoke. After a minute, he rose and turned away. It was the only time that girl ever saw tears welling in a teacher's eyes.

In the lounge he poured himself a cup of coffee, and then sat at his desk and pulled out his books. A sudden wave of spirited singing came from the hallways, and he paused and listened. A group of students were moving along the passage outside in full voice. This apparently spontaneous birth of song lifted his heart, and he held the moment, until the cheap lyrics of the song revealed another paradox. Returning to his things, he packed everything into his briefcase and, as soon as the bell rang, finished his coffee and left for class, hoping to come across Sue on his way, and feeling the early morning might have already offered its full worth.

VII

"Hello Sue, please, do come in." Lilian hugged her warmly and invited her to sit at the small table in the corner of the room by the window overlooking the school gardens. Slices of freshly made sponge cake and a delicate China tea set occupied the middle of the table.

"So nice to get you on your own," said Lilian. "Good to have a heart to heart every now and then." Sue's smile showed she couldn't agree more.

"So, how's it all going?"

Tea and cake were served, and between sips and morsels both women enjoyed the chance to share the smaller, personal things, things which the larger professional issues buried. Keenly aware that were it not for their respective positions she would have welcomed Sue as a very close friend, Lilian took special pleasure in their chats.

Sue was experienced enough to know that behind the genuine affability there must lay a reason for the invitation, but she was in no rush to get to it. A few more minutes passed, while they spoke of the cake, their pets, and the books they were reading.

"How are you getting along with the new teachers? I hear they're a lively bunch," Lilian said.

Such subtlety was not beyond Sue's grasp. She placed her cup carefully back onto the saucer and dabbed the sides of her mouth with a napkin.

"I know," she said. "I mean, I know what you're asking."

Lilian cast her a long, gentle look.

"Yes, I know," Susan continued. "They don't mean any harm, they're just having fun. Actually, I quite like the attention, and not for the wrong reasons, as you might be thinking. I'm not the butt of their jokes. What a terrible expression that is," she said, smiling. "I don't feel like that anyway. When on their own they are quite respectful and I like them, well, two of them. It's just 'boys will be boys' stuff I feel. And to be honest, I do learn things sometimes. Even George has joined in."

"Really? I thought it was only the junior teachers."

Lilian looked at her steadily.

"Oh yes, not often, but he does make me think."

Lilian felt a surge of respect. Sue had been quietly aware all this time, and had a generous perspective on it. Though Lewgh had been right.

Lilian made notes in her diary and in the brief silence, Sue felt deflated. The reason for the chat, she felt, had now come out. Neither pleasantries nor having her feelings about the banter explored were enough. She felt that this would now be the end of the meeting, and she didn't want to leave this corner of Lilian's world with its fine China and comfort cake. She didn't want to have to close the door behind her. Feeling that a deeper bond was being kept at bay by work, she was torn. Deep inside her lay a wish that maybe, once they both retired, a sharing of open hearts without concern would be possible.

Not wanting the chat to end so soon either, Lilian redirected it back to Sue's classes.

"I happened by your class on Tuesday," she said. "I must say, I thought it was excellent. I loved your efforts to encourage them to immerse themselves much more in the experiences they write about. And, by extension, in life itself, I suppose, as Anne mentioned. She was very engaged."

"Oh yes, she always is. They're all darlings, but she's my favourite, I must admit," said Sue.

"Well…they all love you and you love them, but I'm sure Anne deserves that honour. Have you seen any results yet?"

"No, not yet. Deadline is next Tuesday," Sue said. "I would love to show you, if you wish."

"Yes, lovely. In the second break on Tuesday then."

Sue opened her diary and quite unnecessarily wrote it in. The bell sounded. They both stood and hugged again. Lilian opened the door and watched as Sue made her way back to her classroom. On her way out, Sue wondered if she should have said more, or less, about George.

VIII

The massive wooden table occupied most of the centre of the room. This room was adjacent to Lilian's office and suggested a men's club room decorated by women. The seriousness of the oak wall panels and table was relieved by the many colourful flourishes of freshly cut flowers and several paintings of children. Most agreed it was one of the most pleasant rooms in the school. It was 2:40 and sat round the table waiting to start the end of the week meeting were all the teachers, including the latest addition, the Spanish teacher, Jorge Bregos, who had entered the previous Monday.

Never one to arrive late for effect, Lilian passed through the door with her secretary at precisely 2.45pm. Slowly edging around the table, smiling as she passed, she reached the far end and sat down and opened her diary.

"Hello, everyone, many thanks for being on time. We do have a few routine issues to go through, of course, and I'd like to hear from those who wish to speak about whatever is uppermost in their minds." She looked at Nets, and then at the whole group.

"I don't need to remind the ones who have been here before, that respect and openness is essential, so please take that to heart and fear not."

Most of the teachers then briefly glossed over the negative aspects of the week and some embellished the positive. Wise enough to rarely ask if she didn't already know, Lilian wasn't much surprised or taken in by their comments. And when she didn't know, the question often had another purpose.

Nets had been staring down at his clipboard since she had looked at him, and said nothing throughout the meeting. Jorge said nothing either, but listened to the others wide-eyed.
Lilian made a brief note in her diary and then continued.

"Good, good. Now, following our custom, we will end our meeting by asking our newest star to tell us about how he feels. Jorge…if you would."
Although no one else had, Jorge stood up, and in brave, broken English, he began addressing everyone as 'amigo.'

"Sí, sí. You good friends, amigos. Aye, aye, aye."
Taking a deep breath, he continued.
"First days no big problemas. The usual, seguro, but good, muy bien. My amigos here," he said, waving his arm around the group, "is helping me…mucho."
A beautiful smile followed, which warmed the hearts of those listening.

"We're glad to be considered your friends, Jorge. Moochohs grassyus," said Tunrig. Not having been able to display his polyglotism before in public, he plunged further in.

"Todohs somohs amigohs."

Jorge beamed again, and sat down.

Lilian added a second reminder in her diary; to check if Jorge ever spoke in English during class. She then thanked everyone, and they all stood and wished each other a good weekend.

Lilian returned to her office and sat at her desk. This was the one time of the week she preferred dedicating to settling her feelings, which recently had been unusually mixed, rather than to clarifying her thoughts. Overriding all the feelings were those of disappointment, of pleasant surprise, and of uncertainty.

Half an hour later she rose, put her coat and scarf on and walked the grounds, smiling and wishing well to all she passed. Back at her desk, she tucked her belongings into her bag and slid her chair under the desk. She then left the hollow school to wend her way through the weekend ahead.

Still Forked

"So, what did the consultant say?"

"Well, I know what he meant…I've been an idiot and no operation could fix that…things could be worse…but the op will fix it one way or the other…I'll be in the best of hands…blah, blah, blah. God, I hate these people, Alan. How did he think I felt after that? Bloody confused, and scared, that's how. Can always count on you though, Alan. But I can get a taxi, really."

"No, no. No problem, Mike. What a pickle you've gotten yourself into. I am sorry. But still, chin up, as they say. If they do have to…you know…then they'll get you one of those prosthetic ones. The new ones are amazing, I hear. You'll be playing rugby again in no time at all! But it's time, we should be off."

That joke always fails…but I know you feel the same about these places…and you can't really handle disabilities, seem to unnerve you…we'll see how that goes.

"Yes, yes, let's go."

"We're here. Hop out, and wait here for me while I park, and we'll go in together."

"This is your room, Mr Charles. Please take off all your clothes and put on the gown. The open part goes at the back. The nurse will drop by very soon."

"Here…give me your clothes…I'll look after them, and I'll be back after you come round, promise. Cheer up old friend. Fingers crossed."

"Hello, my love. My name's Mary, I'll be lookin' after you today. Ah, good, you put the gown on right. The other way round would cause a bit of a scene, wouldn't it, now? Just gonna check your vitals and hook you up. There, all set. They'll be comin' for you in a tick, so you just lay back and rest a bit."

Does she know?…seems a good sort…nice smile.
"Bye bye, Alan. See you soon. Many thanks."

"One, two, three. There, now off we go. Hang on tight!"

Not so fast…wretched neon lights…like a bloody prison…this must be it…a bit noisy…wonder if they're here yet.

"Hello, Mr Charles. I'm just going to give you a little anaesthesia, and Bob's your uncle."

Why so close?…I'm not deaf…why do eyes always look more attractive above a mask…can't make her accent…no, no he's not…where does that come from…loud voices…must be them…it's the left leg…don't screw up…left!…heard about mistakes like that…awful…

"Morning, Mr Charles. I'm Doctor Andrews, remember? And this is Doctor Rose. In a few moments we'll be starting. No need to worry, you're in the best of hands."

Hope so, so much…so…

"All OK your side, nurse?"

"Yes, doctor."

"Ok, John. Let's get started."

"That's the right leg, nurse, right?"

"No, doctor! Oh…"

"Always gets a reaction. Right, nurse?"

What?...left…left…idiots.

"Ok. Here we go then. All set, John?"

"Yep."

No…

"Did you hear about Phil's final round? Six under par! He was very chuffed."

"Good for him. Maybe drinks later to celebrate?"

"Good idea…this won't take too long. How about your game, John?"

"Couple of bogeys last weekend, but it was hellishly windy. Missed two easy putts too. Caddy chose the wrong iron, he said. The useless bugger."

"Oops! Well, better luck next time."

Oops?

"Oh! Look at this, James. What do you see?"

"Oh, yes. That's odd. The scans didn't show any on that one."

"I don't think so."

"What do you think?"

"There must've been some mistake in radio."

"Oh dear. Hmm..."

Mistake?

"I know, but we can't leave it like this. We have to remove both."

"Yes, yes, you're right."

Both? No!

"Just one of the many problems with this little hospital of ours. More mistakes are made as the budget gets tighter and the equipment gets older. I reckon we might soon have more lawyers here than nurses."

Lawyers?

"Chap's murmering a bit. All OK with you, Mary?"

"Yep, he's fine, James."

"Have you guys heard the one about the cleaner, teacher and lawyer all together at the pearly gates being questioned? Well, I'd change lawyer for hospital administrator."

"Well, our one, anyway. There, both removed."

No!

"Good. Actually, the rest doesn't look that bad, so after I've fixed it, I think we can stop there. I see no real reason to continue. Good bit of work there, John, I must say."

"Yes, that should be enough, at least for a while. Once you finish, I'll close up. To be honest, I don't get much opportunity now with my new practice."

Practice?

"How's that going?"

"Going very well, thanks. Soon be hiring a few more. Did I hear right, James? You're thinking about retiring?"

"Thinking about it, but I'll wait till next year, at least. Got offered a partnership in a small clinic by an old friend of mine, Jeffery Borden. Maybe you heard him last year at the convention."

"I remember him. Nice chap. Damn good convention too, best party ever. Shame about the workshop videos on the plane though. Same ones as last year."

"It was good. Well, he came up to me after, and over drinks he sounded out if I would be interested. I just might be."

Both…no!

"Hang on, bit of loose thread there. There, got it. Well, that's that. Nurse, take these away, and we're done. Now, I have to see what I invent for the op report."

"OK. I'm off. Catch you later, James."

No!

"Mr. Charles, Mr Charles, can you hear me?"

"Yeah…can't…can't..."

"No problem. You're back in your room now. How are you feeling?"

"Gonna…"

"Oh dear. Don't worry, don't worry. The nurse will clean you up. I'll come by a little later."

"There, that's better, my luv...all clean now. You'll be right as rain once the anaesthesia wears off. I'll pop out and get some more water for you. Won't be a tick."

My legs! Christ, you've butchered me! Bastards!

"Didn't take long, did it, luv? I'll put it 'ere next to the bed. Just a few sips at a time. Don't wanna upset your tummy any more, do we, my luv? Don't you fret now, you'll be up and about in no time, you'll see."

"Hello again, Mr Charles, This is Doctor Rose, you might remember him. You should, as thanks to him we avoided the worst."

"What?"

"Yes…yes…Seems there was a confusion about your condition. The infection on the leg wasn't as bad as we first thought, so we removed all the damaged and infected tissue, and fixed a dodgy artery. However, Doctor Rose noticed there was a little complication with the foot, so I'm afraid you lost two toes. Apart from that, it went very well, so we decided to stop there and see how things develop over the next few months. You were moaning a bit, but you were well under. Later, we'll explore the idea of a little reconstructive surgery. If things go well, that might be advisable, but no need to worry about that now. You'll be a bit uncomfortable for a while, and you'll be here for a few weeks, but we'll get you wheelchair till you can get out and about. We've started you on a course of antibiotics, but you must follow your diet and take care to avoid any further lesions! We'll chat much more later, but I hope that's clear for now."

"No…no…you cut my legs off…you…I heard you!"

The doctors gave tired, professional smiles, wished him well, and left.
The nurse sidled up, and, with a tightly held humanity, she tucked him in a little more.

"You're fine, darlin'…lovely pair of legs…for your age anyway," she said, winking and patting his numb right leg.

Acknowledgements

Much gratitude to Amparo Vargas for the photographs, and to Paula Espadas for her illustration of the turtle. Thanks also to AI for the illustration of the grapes.

Peter Kelly was born in England many sunrises ago and spent most of his life in Mexico, where he worked in the field of education. He is a published author of educational books and digital material. He has been writing poetry since he was fourteen only to, much later, witness some of his poems explode into stories, and some of his stories implode into poems. A selection of both is included here, his first published work of non-fiction. He is threatening to publish more, but, as they say in Mexico, 'nunca sabes'.